Catherine
Hapka

Together

SIMON AND SCHUSTER

SIMON AND SCHUSTER

First published in Great Britain by Simon & Schuster UK Ltd, 2005
A Viacom company

Originally published in the USA in 2004 by Aladdin Paperbacks,
an imprint of Simon & Schuster Children's Division, New York.
Copyright © by Catherine Hapka, 2004

1 3 5 7 9 10 8 6 4 2

Simon & Schuster UK Ltd
Africa House
64-78 Kingsway
London WC2B 6AH

A CIP catalogue record for this book is available
from the British Library

ISBN 1416901302

Printed and bound in Great Britain by
Bookmarque Ltd, Croydon, Surrey

One

Star Calloway skipped to the front of the stage. "Okay!" she shouted into her headset, peering past the flashing purple-and-white spotlights at the sea of people beyond. "Anybody want to hear another song from my first album?"

She paused, grinning, as the sold-out crowd roared its approval. Star was a little over halfway through the first of her three concerts in Stockholm, Sweden. The pretty northern European city was the latest stop on Star's first world tour, which had already visited London, Edinburgh, Milan, and Rome. Although the cities she had visited so far were all very different from one another, Star had found that they all had one thing in common – they were packed with fans who couldn't wait to hear her sing.

"Great!" Star cried, stepping back into position at the front of a wedge of background dancers. She'd practised the move so much that she didn't even have to glance over her shoulder anymore to make sure she was in the right spot. "I want you to sing along, okay? This is a song called 'Girl Talk'."

The people in the crowd erupted into a frenzy of joy, stomping their feet on their chairs and shrieking their excitement. 'Girl Talk' had been Star's first worldwide number-one hit – it was the song that had shot her straight to superstardom a year earlier at the age of thirteen, changing her life forever.

Star glanced over at her band at the side of the stage and nodded. Instantly the bouncy opening notes of the song poured out over the giant speakers. For a moment the music was barely audible over the screams and whistles of the audience, but Star and her dancers didn't need to hear the music clearly to know what to do. They began to dance, their arms and legs moving in unison.

On cue, Star stopped dancing and stepped forward. As her background dancers continued their energetic moves behind her, she took a deep breath and sang out the familiar opening lines of the song, her voice pouring out over the speakers, sounding clear and strong.

Even over the huge speakers facing her, she could hear the audience singing along. She was still a little amazed at how well the European audiences spoke – and sang – English. It made her feel a little sheepish about speaking only one language herself, and she had already asked her full-time tutor, Mrs Magdalene Nattle – better known to the rest of the team as Mags – to start incorporating some foreign language lessons into her schoolwork. She also planned to start paying more attention to her driver and head bodyguard, Tank Massimo, who spoke more than a dozen languages fluently.

When there was a break in the lyrics, Star stepped smoothly back into line and started dancing again. As she glanced upwards she noticed a cameraman clambering around overhead in the rigging that held the lights and other equipment. She had been noticing that cameraman and several others throughout the entire show. They were there to shoot footage for Star's next video, which was being directed by the famously eccentric Swedish director Lukas Lukas. Star hadn't met him yet, but she was scheduled to visit his Stockholm studio the following afternoon.

After the break Star stepped forward again. At the first couple of shows she had found herself a little breathless at this point, but thanks to Tank, who acted as her personal trainer as well as her bodyguard and driver, she was in better shape now than when she'd started the tour. Her voice was steady and strong as she sang the final verse.

The musicians moved into the extra instrumental section that had been added to the song just for the tour. The background dancers moved towards the front of the stage, continuing to perform a series of increasingly fast and intricate moves that soon had the audience cheering wildly. But this time Star didn't join in. It was time for her next costume change, and that meant every second counted.

She raced backstage, dodging another cameraman. A small canvas tent, better known as the quick-change booth, had been set up just out of sight of the audience.

Pushing aside the tent's canvas flap, Star leaped inside. Though the quick-change booth was only about the size of a highway tollbooth, there were three people inside waiting for her. One was Lola LaRue, a permanent member of Star's team who was in charge of Star's hair, make-up, and costumes. The other, younger women were assistants Lola had hired to help her during the tour. The booth was also crammed with racks of clothing and boxes of shoes and accessories. It looked like a mess, but somehow Lola always knew exactly where everything was.

Though Lola herself normally favoured funky outfits involving huge feather boas and outrageous hats, she kept her look more streamlined when she was working backstage.

That night she was wearing a simple black T-shirt and a pair of leopard-print stretch leggings. Clips, safety pins, and extra bits of string and Velcro hung from the apron tied around her waist, while make-up brushes and hair spray stuck out of the pockets.

"Sounding good out there tonight, babydoll," Lola said calmly, her nimble fingers already unfastening the hooks at the back of Star's top.

"Thanks," Star said breathlessly, kicking off her shoes. "It's a cool audience."

Lola grinned. "You say that about every audience."

Star slipped out of her shirt, tossed it over a clothes rack, and straightened the straps of the leotard she was wearing underneath. "It's always true!"

Meanwhile one of the assistants was trying to loosen the ties of Star's retro-style macramé belt. "Hey, this thing is all tangled up," the assistant said after a moment, sounding slightly panicky.

Star glanced down and saw that the beaded ends of the belt were tangled and knotted, probably thanks to that last dance number. She gulped, realizing that until she got the belt off, she wouldn't be able to get her skirt off either. "Uh-oh," she said. "Here, let me try – my fingers are smaller."

She picked at the knot, but the strands stubbornly refused to yield. Star gritted her teeth and kept trying, hardly noticing as Lola expertly touched up her make-up.

"I can't get it either!" Star cried at last. "What are we going to do? My cue is in, like, thirty seconds!"

Lola finished fluffing Star's hair. "Don't fret, sugar," she said, her voice as calm as ever. "Move your hands."

Star did as she said. Lola fished in her apron pockets and pulled out a pair of large, shiny steel scissors. With one snip the belt came loose.

Breathing a sigh of relief, Star slipped off her skirt and pulled on the glittery pink dress that was her outfit for the next few songs. "Thanks, Lola," she said gratefully. "You're the best!"

"I know." Lola smiled and zipped up Star's dress, then gave her a quick pat on the shoulder. "Now get back out there and bring it home, okay?"

Star heard her band play the opening notes of the next song. She pushed her way out of the quick-change booth, pausing for a half-second at the edge of the stage to catch her breath and wait for her cue.

Nearby she saw a pair of background dancers crouched in position and waiting for their turn. They were Rachel and

Erin Maxwell, identical twins who, at just eighteen years old, were the youngest dancers on the tour. They were both lively and fun, with reddish-blonde hair. Star hadn't known them very well when the tour started, but after more than three weeks of travelling together she was starting to think of them as good friends.

As Star took a deep breath, knowing that her cue was coming in just a few seconds, one of the twins glanced over and gave her a quick wink, while the other waggled her eyebrows slightly. Star grinned and gave them a thumbs-up.

Then she straightened her headset. A sound technician had switched it off by remote control as soon as she left the stage, and now she could hear by the soft crackle in her earpiece that it was back on and ready to go.

When her cue came, she leaped back onstage and fell into step with the dancers. The audience spotted her immediately and howled with excitement. Star grinned, her entire body pulsing with energy and happiness as she opened her mouth to sing again.

"Okay, gotta go," Star cried, waving to the audience as the final notes of her recent number-one hit song "Supernova" faded away. "You've been awesome! Thank you! I love Sweden!"

The crowd's enthusiastic cheers followed her off the stage. She was exhausted after the strenuous performance, but there was a happy skip in her step as she headed backstage, waving cheerfully to yet another of Lukas Lukas's cameramen. Although the stage itself looked gorgeous and glamorous, with a pretty set that included all sorts of glitter, fabric, and frills, the backstage area was much more utilitarian. It was mostly concrete and drywall, with wiring and other equipment scattered everywhere.

Peeling off her headset and handing it to a passing tech, Star hopped over an extension cord and headed towards a doorway with six-inch-high red letters spelling out a message in Swedish. Below that, someone had taped a cardboard sign reading WARNING: RED PASS REQUIRED FOR ADMITTANCE in English and Swedish. A tall, burly security guard with curly reddish-blond hair was standing beside the doorway casting a stern eye on anyone who approached. When Star approached, his expression changed to a smile.

"*Hejdå,* Miss Calloway," he said.

Star returned his smile. "Goodnight, Erik."

She stepped through the doorway and turned down the brightly lit hallway that contained the series of boxy, concrete-walled rooms that performers used as dressing rooms. Several people called greetings and congratulations as she walked, and Star responded with a quick wave and smile.

Her manager, Mike Mosley, was waiting for her just outside her dressing room along with Lola and Tank. Mike was a tall man with a bushy mustache and intelligent green eyes. He had guided Star's career from the beginning, and Star knew that she wouldn't be a world-famous fourteen-year-old superstar without him. More importantly, she didn't know what she would have done without his strong, comforting presence on the fateful day almost two years earlier when she'd heard that her parents and baby brother had disappeared during a holiday boat trip, or during the difficult, lonely time since then when almost everyone except Star and her team seemed to have given up on ever finding them again.

"Nice job tonight, sweetheart," Mike said in his slow Texas drawl. "They loved you out there. As usual."

"Thanks!" Star stood on the toes of Mike's purple cowboy boots, reaching up as far as she could to give him a hug.

She heard a sharp bark behind her. Turning, she saw that Tank was holding her dog, a chubby fawn pug named Dudley Do-Wrong. Tank was about a foot shorter than Mike but almost twice as wide, with muscles everywhere. He could intimidate a pushy photographer or subdue an over-eager fan with a stern look or a flex of his beefy biceps, but at the moment it seemed to be taking most of his strength to hold on to Dudley. The little pug was wriggling mightily to get free, his tongue lolling out of his flat face as he stared at Star with his bulging eyes.

"Dudster!" Star cried, reaching out to take the little dog from Tank. "Come on, Duds, you can help me change."

Lola rolled her eyes. The stylist had traded her make-up apron for a purple fake-fur stole, and a vintage military beret was perched atop her cornrowed hair.

"Great," Lola said dryly. "With Dudley helping, it'll only take you twice as long as usual. I'd better come along and help."

Star giggled. "Okay," she said. "And I promise I won't let Dudley lick off my make-up this time. At least not all of it."

Despite Lola's prediction, it was only a short time before Star was stepping out of her dressing room wearing jeans and a T-shirt, with her curly blonde hair pulled back into a ponytail.

"Looks like the guys must've already headed out to get the car," Lola commented.

The backstage area was still bustling – various techs were

moving and adjusting the sound equipment, Lola's assistants were dismantling the canvas quick-change booth, and various other people were dashing here and there, while several of Lukas Lukas's cameramen wandered around filming it all. But Mike and Tank were nowhere in sight.

"Come on, let's go find them," Star said, smothering a yawn. She wasn't wearing a watch, but she knew it had to be close to midnight. It had been a long, busy day, and she couldn't wait to get back to the hotel and fall into the luxurious feather bed in her room.

As she followed Lola towards the exit she heard a soft, slightly shy male voice call out her name. She turned to see a handsome teenage boy hurrying through the open door of one of the other dressing rooms. His slightly damp hair was so blond it was almost white, making his bright blue eyes all the more startling. He was wearing jeans and a plain white undershirt, his feet were bare, and a towel was slung around his neck.

"Oh, hi, Sven!" Star exclaimed happily. "I was hoping I'd run into you. I only heard the last half of your set tonight, but you were totally awesome! I'm so glad you agreed to open for me here in Stockholm."

The boy looked slightly overwhelmed by her enthusiasm.

"Oh, no, Star," he said in heavily accented English. "It is you who is awesome. It is my honour to sing before your concert show."

Star smiled at him. She had never heard of Sven Studborg when Mike had signed him as her opening act on the Swedish leg of the tour. The young singer had just released his first album in his home country, and he was so popular there and throughout Scandinavia that his record company was already talking about a second album to be recorded in English for international release.

"Thanks, Sven." Star scanned her mind, trying to remember the Swedish phrase of thanks she'd heard Tank use several times since arriving in Stockholm. "Er, I mean *tack so mucket*."

Sven chuckled. "That is said *tack så mycket*," he corrected. "And you are most welcome."

Star giggled. "Oops," she said. "Guess it will be a while before my Swedish is as good as your English. But I love your language – it's so pretty and interesting-sounding! In fact, I love just about everything here so far."

"My country, it admires you greatly as well," Sven said. "As do I. Your music, it is my favourite of all the American acts. I especially like the new song named 'Over the Top'."

"Really?" Star's heart jumped. The song Sven mentioned was really special to her. It was one of several that Star had co-written for her second album, her first attempts at song-writing. She thought it had turned out pretty well, but she still held her breath anxiously every time anyone mentioned it, from music reviewers and PopTV VJs to ordinary fans.

Lola had returned from checking the doorway just in time to hear the last part of the conversation. She put an arm around Star's shoulders and squeezed. "You have a good ear, Sven," she said. "Our little Star here has a real knack for songwriting. She's a natural! Practically a shoo-in for the next songwriting Notey Award, don't you think?"

Star blushed as Sven looked slightly confused. Lola was a loyal friend – so loyal that she had a habit of occasionally exaggerating Star's abilities and accomplishments. At least this time there was no one around to hear it except Star and Sven. Lola had been the object of Mike's ire more than once for gushing too enthusiastically about Star to the press.

"I don't know about that, Lola," Star said quickly. "But writing songs is way fun. I always thought nothing could be as cool as singing and dancing for an audience. But writing 'Over the Top' and the other songs is like a whole different kind of thing."

Sven nodded enthusiastically. "Yes, yes, exactly right," he said. "When I am writing my music, it is like I am in a different place. Time has no meaning, and I am lost in the world inside my head, where I can hear the music as if it is already complete."

"That's perfect!" Star exclaimed. "You know, for someone who speaks mostly Swedish, you really have a talent with the English language!"

Sven's cheeks turned pink and he grinned bashfully. "I thank you, Star. You are too kind."

There was a sharp buzz, and Lola pulled a mobile phone out from under her purple stole. She checked the number. "That's Mike," she told Star. "He must be calling from the car."

As Lola put the phone to her ear Star turned back to Sven. "Guess that means I've got to go," she said. "Sorry! I wish we could keep talking about this."

"It is so nice for me to talk with you, as well." Sven sounded shy again. "It is – um, how do you say it? It is difficult for me, you know, now that I am well-known here in Sweden. It is difficult to know if persons are truly wanting to be a friend with me, or if they are wanting to know me because of my fame. Even my old manager, I would wonder about such things." He blushed slightly. "I am sorry for my bad English. I hope you can understand my meaning?"

"Yes," Star assured him. "I know just what you mean."

"Ah, that is so good to hear." Sven smiled. "I – I wonder, Star. That is, I know you are busy. Would you possibly have the time for having lunch with me tomorrow? Of course, I will understand if your schedule will not allow this."

He looked so anxious that Star almost laughed. "That sounds great!" she said. "I'll have my manager call yours and set something up if at all possible. Okay?"

"That is wonderful!" Sven looked pleased. Just then a tall, dark-haired man appeared in the doorway of Sven's dressing room and called to him in Swedish. "Ah, but now I must let you go," Sven said. "That is my new manager – he is telling me I must take an interview on the phone now. I am sorry to cut this short."

"That's okay," Star said. "I totally understand. I hope we can talk more tomorrow at lunch."

Sven smiled. "Good! Then I bid you goodnight."

"Goodnight," Star replied as he hurried off.

Star yawned and stared out the window as Tank steered her limo through the huge iron gates of the hotel grounds. Star and her entourage were staying at a brand-new, super-luxurious spa resort that had recently opened in the outskirts of Stockholm. Star, Lola, Mike, Tank and Mags were staying in a large private villa set within a secluded walled courtyard complete with hot tub, lap pool, and meditation garden. The rest of the entourage — dancers, musicians, techs, roadies, publicists, and assorted others — were housed in a cluster of smaller villas nearby.

Soon the car pulled to a stop in front of the villa. Star yawned again as she unhooked her seat belt. But despite her body's exhaustion, her mind still felt wide awake. She wondered if anyone else from the tour felt the same way — maybe some of the dancers would feel like hanging out for a while.

"I'm kind of wired," she commented as she climbed out of the limo. "I wonder if Rachel and Erin are still up?"

Mike glanced at his watch as Tank unlocked the villa's courtyard gate, which was a smaller version of the iron entrance gate. "Dunno," he said. "But I'd suggest you don't bother to find out. It's late, and you need to catch some z's if you're going to get everything done tomorrow."

Star realized he was right. She had mentioned Sven's lunch invitation to Mike in the car, and her manager had agreed to squeeze it into her already busy schedule.

Oh well, she thought. *I guess I can hang out with Rachel and Erin some other time.*

Despite her slight disappointment, she couldn't help feeling a twinge of relief as well. Star was naturally outgoing and rarely bothered by shyness, but she felt a little weird about just calling up the twins to see if they wanted to hang out with her. They were eighteen years old – four whole years older than Star – and she really didn't know them that well yet.

They might not be all that thrilled about hanging with someone my age, she thought as she walked down the short granite and gravel path between the gate and the front door. *Then again, maybe they'd feel like they had to, just because of their jobs or who I am or . . .*

She bit her lip, remembering Sven's comments earlier about not knowing who his real friends were. That was one of the hardest things she'd found about being famous. She'd learned that some people had trouble seeing past the fame, glamour, and fortune to the real, live girl behind it all. Were the Maxwell twins that way? Star doubted it – but she couldn't really be sure.

Tank unlocked the villa's front door, and Star followed the adults into the main room. It was a large, soaring space furnished with ultramodern chairs, sofas, and tables of pale wood and gleaming chrome. Soft geometric carpets covered the polished pine floors, and the stucco walls were painted in soothing shades of beige and pale green.

Mags was sitting on one of the angular sofas reading a book and drinking a cup of tea. She was in her sixties, with short-cropped salt-and-pepper hair and a no-nonsense manner that commanded instant respect.

"How was the show tonight?" Mags asked, setting aside her book.

"Great!" Star said. "The crowd was really cool. Oh, and you have to meet Sven, my opening act. You'll love him – he's super smart and thoughtful and stuff."

"And quite the little hottie, too," Lola put in. "Too bad I'm not about twenty years younger." She grinned and winked.

Star giggled and rolled her eyes. "Please don't forget to call Sven's manager, okay, Mike?" she said as she kicked off her shoes near the door. "It was so nice of Sven to invite me to lunch – he seems really sweet. I'm glad he's opening for me."

Mike nodded. "He turned out to be a solid choice," he said. "Good singer, good kid. It's nice to give talented local acts a break when we can. Besides, his new manager is a friend of a friend." He shook his head. "That kid's lucky he got hooked up with a pro like that at this point in his career.

I hear his old manager was a real flake. Young Sven could've wasted a heap of time and talent without ever really goin' anywhere."

Star grinned. "Mike, is that your way of reminding me to be thankful for having such a super-talented, amazingly skilled manager like you helping my career?"

Tank, Lola, and Mags laughed as Mike's face turned red. "Not at all," he muttered uncomfortably from behind his mustache. He cleared his throat. "Now listen, let's not stand around here yappin' all night. Time to get some rest, y'all."

Soon everyone was scattering towards the kitchen, the bathroom, or his or her own bedroom. Star said goodnight to her team and wandered up the spiral staircase to her room.

When she entered, she immediately glanced at the comfortable expanse of the room's king-size bed. But she was still feeling too restless to go straight to sleep. Sitting down on the edge of her bed, she tapped her fingers on the end table, still pondering her earlier thoughts. Why had she felt so awkward at the idea of calling Rachel and Erin to get together? After being on tour together for so many weeks, practising steps and laughing at silly inside jokes, she was pretty sure they were all becoming real friends. She always had a blast hanging out with them and the rest of the dancers as a group. Why should it be any different to want to spend some time with just the twins, like regular friends getting together?

Oh well, she thought at last. *Whatever the Maxwell twins and the other dancers think of me, I know there are people back home who have always truly liked me for who I am, not what I do or how much money I have.*

She could almost hear her best friend, Missy Takamori, snort and say *Darn right!* to that. Smiling at the thought, Star jumped to her feet and hurried over to the dresser where her laptop was sitting. She carried it over to the bed. Sitting down cross-legged on the plush comforter, she booted up and quickly typed out an e-mail, her fingers flying over the small keyboard.

From: singingstar01

To: MissTaka

Subject: Whatevah . . .

Yo Missy,

Howz it going gf? I'm still in Sweden. (Duh! Hasn't changed since I wrote 2 U like six hours ago!!!) U would luv it here — there r lotsa cute boyz, & all the peeps are sooooo nice!

NEwayz, it's late & I just finished a show. It was fun. U would like my opening act here — his name is Sven, & he's super sweet. He's only a few yrs older than us, and he's a big * here in Sweden, but he's totally down 2 earth and stuff. I'm having lunch w/him 2morrow.

2morrow's also when I meet w/Lukas Lukas. I can't wait 2 meet him — everyı sez he's totally wacko! But also, like, a genius or something. That video he did 4 Eddie Urbane last year rocked! I hope mine turns out 2b just as cool.

Guess I'd better sleep now. Be sure to tell Nans I'm OK and I miss her. Also say hi 4 me to Mandy and Shayla and Ash and the rest of the New Limpet Middle School gang, okay? Oh, and Aaron 2, of course . . . I miss all u guys! (But esp. *U*!!)

Luv and stuff,

Star

Star hit SEND and sat back on the bed. As the computer's tiny clock spun, timing her message's delivery, she wondered what Missy was doing right that minute back home in Pennsylvania. As she tried to picture her friend's face, Star was hit with a sudden wave of homesickness. She was usually so busy that she didn't have time to think about how long she'd been gone. She had already scheduled a visit home during an upcoming break in the tour, which coincided with her grandmother's birthday. But that visit was more than two weeks away – and suddenly two weeks seemed like an eternity.

As the computer let out a soft beep, letting Star know that her e-mail had been delivered, Star pulled it towards her again. Not stopping to think about what she was doing, she impulsively typed out another message to Missy.

From: singingstaro1

To: MissTaka

Subject: ps . . .

Me again . . .

Listen, I just had an awesome idea. It's summer holidays there, right? And I'm dying 2 see u and my other buds from home. So y don't u all come visit me?? I'm talking u, Aaron, Shayla, Ash, Trina, Mandy – whoever can make it from the usual gang. (I would say 2 bring Nans along, but we all know that's hopeless – I don't think she really believes planes can actually fly! Ha ha!)

NEwayz, I have a whole day off between my 2nd and 3rd concerts here (except 4 a few interviews & stuff), so that would be the best time 2 come. U guys could plan 2 fly here the day after 2morrow, and stay 4 my last Stockholm show.

Don't worry about the $$$, either. Just yesterday Mike was saying I spend way less on tour than any other celeb he's ever met. So he prolly won't mind if I bring u guys here! It's the best way I can think of 2 spend all this $$ they tell me the tour is making!

So what do u say? Sounds like fun, right??? Mike could make all the arrangements and stuff; all u guys have 2 do is say the word.

Let me know ASAP, OK?

Star

Two

The next morning Star awoke to the scent of bacon wafting in beneath the bedroom door. Yawning widely, she sat up and rubbed her eyes. Bright sunlight was pouring into the room through the cracks in the blinds, letting her know that she'd slept much later than usual.

Thanks, Mike, she thought gratefully, realizing that her manager must have shuffled some of her morning appointments to allow her to sleep in. That was just one of the reasons he was such a great manager – he often seemed to sense exactly what Star needed even before she realized it herself.

Climbing out of bed, Star pulled on a robe and hurried out of her room, her stomach rumbling hungrily. As she reached the stairs she heard the sound of voices from below.

She hurried down the winding steps. Nearing the bottom, she saw that several people were seated at the oval dining table in front of the picture window at one end of the room:

Mike, Lola, Tank, and Tricia Moore, one of the publicists Mike had hired at the start of the tour. Tricia was a fortyish woman with vibrant, stylishly short magenta hair and bright red lipstick. She was wearing a chic trousersuit and holding a thick manila folder.

"Morning, everyone," Star said. "Hi, Tricia. When did you get in?"

The publicist glanced up and gave Star a dazzling smile. "Star, darling!" she cried in a thick New York accent, her words firing rapidly out of her bright red mouth. "You know I can't stay away from you for long. Especially when your tour is getting reviews like this!" She held up her manila folder and waved it vigorously. Several newspaper clippings flew out and went floating down onto the geometric-patterned rug.

Mike bent to retrieve one of the clippings, which had landed near his left boot. "Tricia flew in from London this morning," he told Star. "She'll be helpin' us out with a couple of interviews over the next few days."

"Oh. That's nice." Star glanced at the empty plates on the table and sniffed hopefully at the air. "Is there any more bacon?"

"Mags figured you'd be up soon. She just went in to fry up

some more," Lola replied, cocking a thumb towards a hallway at one end of the room. "She's in heaven now that we're finally staying in a place with a real kitchen. I just hope she doesn't expect us all to pitch in with the dishes!"

The entire group laughed except for Tricia, who was busily flipping through the articles in her folder. "Star! Darling!" she cried abruptly. "I wanted you to see this. Come over here, darling."

Star obeyed, padding across the carpet to stand beside Tricia. She hadn't spent much time with the publicist – Mike usually handled that end of things – but she already knew that when Tricia spoke, it was easiest just to do as she said.

The publicist whipped out a clipping from a glossy magazine. The article featured a picture of Star, along with several other young music stars including Eddie Urbane, Jade, the members of the hot boy band Boysterous, and others.

"There you are, front and centre, biggest picture on the page!" Tricia said proudly, stabbing at the photo with a long red fingernail. "See? They mention here that you'll be filming your next video with Lukas Lukas, and that he's thrilled at the chance to work with you. Quite a coup!" She shot a quick glare in Lola's general direction. "Believe me, darling, it took some doing to get the magazine people to believe that was a real quote from Lukas after a certain someone told one of their reporters that the pope had personally recommended Star's albums to everyone he knew."

"I never said he recommended them," Lola put in calmly. "I said he probably *would* recommend them if he heard them."

Mike rolled his eyes. "Never mind that," he said gruffly. "Thanks, Tricia. Gettin' that spread in *Gloss* magazine was real good work."

Tricia beamed. "I totally agree, if I do say so myself. Everyone loves this kind of publicity – any kind of publicity, really!" She barked out a laugh, then glanced at her diamond-studded watch. "Oops, I've got to dash. I'm supposed to be downtown ten minutes ago. *Ciao,* everyone!"

"*Ciao,* Tricia," Tank replied pleasantly. "*Era bello per vederti questa mattina.*"

Tricia looked slightly confused. "Uh-huh," she said. "Later, people." With a quick wave, she grabbed her manila folder and hurried towards the door.

"Wow," Star murmured as the door swung shut behind Tricia. "After that, I think I'm ready to go back to bed."

Lola snorted with laughter. "I hear you, babydoll," she said. "I think if someone held that woman's mouth shut for more than ten seconds, she'd explode."

Star giggled. Tricia was nice enough, but she didn't quite fit in with her laid-back, down-to-earth core group.

Mike smiled. "Tricia can talk the horns off a billy goat," he admitted. "But she's a darned good publicist, and that's what matters."

Star nodded quickly, feeling guilty about making fun of Tricia. "Sorry, Mike," she said. "You're totally right, as always. Tricia is awesome at her job."

"Anybody out here hungry?"

Star turned to see her tutor hurrying in from the kitchen carrying a steaming plate of bacon and eggs. Dudley was trotting along at Mags's feet, his bulging eyes trained on the plate.

"Yum!" Star cried. "Please say that's for me, because I'm starved!"

Mags raised an eyebrow. "Oh?" she said. "Starved, really?"

Star knew that her tutor was a stickler for accuracy – among her pet peeves were exaggeration and sloppy language. Mags had just about given up on correcting Lola's frequent overstatements, but she still had hopes for Star.

"Well, maybe not quite *starved*," Star admitted. "Let's just say very, very, very hungry."

"All right." Mags seemed mollified by that. She set the plate down in front of Star and smiled. "Dig in."

Star was happy to oblige. As she ate, Mike pulled out one of the notebooks he always carried with him and began going over her schedule for the day.

"I pushed back that print interview to later this afternoon," he said. "That means you just have to do the TV spot and a short meet-and-greet and photo op with our Swedish distributors before your lunch with Sven. I'm afraid you won't have a whole lot of time to hang out. Your meeting with Lukas Lukas is at two, and I hear he hates when performers stroll in late."

Star swallowed a bite of eggs. "I'm sort of nervous about meeting him," she confessed. "But I also sort of can't wait. A couple of the dancers have worked with him before, and they said he's totally wacked out!"

"Hmm." Mike looked amused. "I suppose you could call him eccentric. He has all the tact of a coonhound on a scent, he won't work with anyone if he doesn't like their aura, and he generally looks like two hundred miles of bad road. But he knows what he's doing in the editing room. That video he did for Urbane last winter racked up more awards than you could shake a stick at."

"Yeah," Lola put in, pilfering a piece of Star's bacon and popping it into her mouth. "And it was really cool, too."

Before Star could respond, the shrill ring of a mobile phone interrupted. Mike fished a phone out of his shirt pocket and flipped it open. "Mosley here," he said. "Oh, hey there, Tricia."

"She can't be more than twenty feet away from the front door," Lola whispered. "What the heck does she have to call us about al-freakin'-ready?"

Mike held up a hand, listening. Then he glanced over at Tank. "Flip on the tube," he said. "Quick. PopTV."

Tank jumped up and hurried over to the low-slung coffee table. Grabbing the remote, he switched on the large-screen TV tucked into a modular entertainment unit against one wall.

A "breaking news" graphic was flashing at the bottom of the screen, and above it was a photo of a pretty, pouty teenage girl.

"Hey, that's Jade," Star said, recognizing her fellow teen pop idol. The two of them had met for the first time a few weeks earlier in London. Star had liked Jade at first – at least until Jade and her entourage had told the world about Star's missing family, a secret Mike and the rest of Star's team had carefully kept for almost two years. Now Star wasn't quite sure what to think of her.

" . . . and word is that both sides are looking forward to the project, and to their meeting in Stockholm this week," a VJ's voice was saying as Jade's latest hit song played in the background. "This removes any doubt that Lukas Lukas is becoming the director of choice for the world's hottest young acts."

With that, the screen split and a picture of a grumpy-looking, shaggy-haired man appeared beside Jade's photo. Star recognized Lukas Lukas from other pictures she'd seen of him.

"So Jade is doing a video with Lukas, too?" Lola sounded miffed. "Copycat!"

Mike shrugged. "No big surprise," he said. "She's hardly the only one who wants to work with him. Lukas is going to be as busy as he wants to be for the next little while."

"Right," Tank agreed. "At least until somebody else becomes the next big thing."

As Star looked up from slipping Dudley a scrap of bacon, she saw her own face appear on the screen. She blinked in surprise. "Hey, there I am."

The photo showed Star singing onstage. This time the VJ, a young man with a nose ring and a shaved head, appeared in front of it. "Speaking of Stockholm," he said, "we've just heard that Star Calloway's concert tour landed there last night and was a smash success."

The picture changed, flashing to a different shot of Star. This one showed her standing with Sven Studborg.

"But that's not all," the VJ went on. "Recent romantic rumours linked the fresh-faced pop princess with fellow superstar Eddie Urbane. When Eddie turned out to be involved with new age guru Xandra Om, we all feared that poor Star might be suffering a broken heart. But now, reliable sources tell PopTV that America's sweetheart has found a Swedish sweetie of her own – hunky teen singer Sven Studborg, who is opening for Star while she's in Stockholm. We wish them all the best as they make beautiful music together!"

Star gasped. "Hey!" she exclaimed. "That's so not true! Sven and I are just friends. Besides, we only met, like, forty-eight hours ago – how are we supposed to be some kind of couple already?"

Tank shrugged as he switched off the sound on the TV and returned to his seat at the table. "Hey, that'd be more than enough time for Eddie Urbane," he joked.

Mike snorted. "True enough," he grumbled. "Don't fret,

sweetheart. It's just another silly rumour. You have to let it roll off your back."

"Yeah, I know." Star sighed, her annoyance already fading. She still didn't understand how reporters could make up stories about people just because they were famous, and how so many people could believe them without an ounce of proof. But she was getting used to it. Besides, she couldn't help seeing the humour in this particular piece of gossip, which had her dating a boy with whom she'd spent a grand total of about ten minutes.

"Next thing you know, I'll be dumping poor Sven for that bellboy who carried our stuff when we checked in," she said with a giggle. "Or maybe Erik, the security guard at the stadium last night . . . he's a little old for me, but I think he might be my soul mate."

Tank, Mike, and Mags laughed, but Lola was still glaring at the TV. "Speaking of Eddie Urbane," the stylist said grimly, "how much do you wanna bet that he's behind this rumour?"

Mags blinked at her in surprise. "The Urbane boy?" she said. "How do you figure?"

"She could be right." Tank shrugged. "We already know Urbane will do just about anything to keep his name in the news. If someone told him about Sven opening for Star, well . . . let's just say it wouldn't be the first less-than-honest thing he's done."

Star grimaced and glanced at Mike to see what he thought. Her manager was stroking his mustache thoughtfully and staring at the TV, which was now showing a commercial for basketball shoes.

"Mike?" she said. "Do you think Eddie might've planted the rumour about me and Sven?"

Mike didn't answer for a moment. "That photo," he murmured. "Did y'all see it?"

"Of course." Lola shrugged. "What do you think we've been talking about all this time?"

Mike didn't seem to notice her sarcasm. "I can't believe that shot of you two was up there," he muttered grimly.

Star was surprised that he suddenly seemed so upset. "What's the big?" she asked. "You just finished telling me this is just another rumour, blah blah blah."

"That was before I realized that photo wasn't from your first meeting with Sven at the press conference the day we arrived," Mike said, meeting her gaze at last. His green eyes were troubled. "It was from backstage, last night after the concert."

"So?" Star asked.

Tank gasped. "You're right!" he exclaimed. "How did PopTV get their hands on something like that? The backstage area was supposed to be closed to anyone except our own people. Oh, and the Lukas Lukas cameras, of course. But they wouldn't pull something like this – would they?"

Mike was already pulling out his phone. "I'd better check in with Tricia," he murmured. "She might've misunderstood something, given permission to Lukas's guys or someone else to release that photo . . ."

Everyone at the table waited silently while Mike dialled. They could all hear Tricia's voice clearly as she answered a second later.

"It's me," Mike said into the phone. Before he could go on, a torrent of words erupted from the phone, though Star couldn't understand what Tricia was saying. "Yes, yes, we saw it," Mike went on after a moment. "But listen – about that photo . . ."

He quickly explained the problem. Once again, Tricia's tinny voice poured through the phone's tiny speaker.

Mike frowned into the phone. "Glad to hear it wasn't you, Tricia," he said. "But listen, it's *not* a blessing in disguise, okay? Star is fourteen years old – we don't need to be happy for any more rumours about her romantic life."

He hung up and glanced around the table. Tank cleared his throat. "Guess that means she wasn't behind it, huh?"

"Nope." Mike shook his head grimly. "Had no idea. She's going to check in with the Lukas camp, but she's pretty sure they wouldn't do something like that. So it seems we've got a photo sniper on our hands."

Star shuddered. It was one thing to have photographers chasing her around whenever she appeared in public. But it was more than a little creepy to think that someone had been snapping pictures of her during what she'd thought was a relaxed private moment. She picked up Dudley and set him on her lap, hugging him tightly. He wriggled impatiently, his gaze locked on the leftover bacon on her plate.

"I still think Eddie is behind it," Lola said. "He could've sent a spy in or something. With his connections, he'd be able to figure out a way."

Mike didn't look convinced. "Seems a little far-fetched, even for Urbane." He glanced at Star. "But like I said, it's nothing for you to fret about. It was probably a fluke. If not, I'll get to the bottom of it soon enough."

*

By the time she climbed into the limo to head to lunch, Star had almost forgotten about the new rumour. In her short career so far, she had been the subject of countless false or misleading news stories. There had been the time near the beginning of her career that a newspaper story had claimed that Star was twenty-three years old rather than thirteen. Not long after, a national teen magazine had reported that Star's beauty routine included rubbing raw fish on her skin. More recently, Lola had accidentally told a New York radio personality that Star was quitting show business. And of course, there had been the most devastating news flash of all, although that one had been all too true – when Jade had leaked the truth about Star's missing family to the press.

Even that had turned out all right in the end, though. Now that the whole world knew about Star's family's disappearance, she was sure it was only a matter of time before someone found them. And when that happened, the media could spread all the false rumours they wanted – Star would be far too happy to notice.

"Is this the place?" she asked Tank, peering out the window as the limo slowed to a crawl on a busy shop-lined street in the centre of Stockholm.

Tank nodded and swung the steering wheel towards the

curb. "Apparently this is young Sven's favourite restaurant. Mike arranged to clear it out for the next hour so you two could have some peace and privacy."

"Really?" Star pretended to pout. "Hey, if Sven and I are going to be the only ones there, then why wasn't I allowed to bring Dudley? He loves Swedish food."

Tank grinned. "And French food, and Chinese food, and American food, and British food, and Italian food, and Indian food . . ."

Sven was waiting for Star just inside the restaurant, which was decorated with traditional Scandinavian accents. "*Hej,* Star! I am so happy you still are coming!" he cried, hurrying forward to greet her. "I was so afraid – after the story report on the television – well . . ."

Star laughed. "You mean that silly story about us?" She waved one hand. "Don't even worry about it. People say stuff like that about me all the time. I just hope *you* weren't upset by it."

"Of course, no," Sven said earnestly. "But I did not want you to think that I or my people . . ." He paused helplessly, obviously struggling for words.

Star gestured towards Tank, who was standing behind her. "If you're having trouble, Tank speaks Swedish."

"Ah! Wonderful!" Sven turned to Tank and said something in his own language.

Tank nodded. "Star, Sven says he hopes you don't think that he or his people had anything to do with the rumours," he translated. "He wants you to know that he respects you too much as a person and a friend ever to do anything to hurt you."

"Oh! That's so sweet." Star smiled at Sven. "Don't worry, I didn't think that for a second."

Sven looked relieved. "Oh, that is very good!" he exclaimed. "But come, let us sit down. This restaurant, it is very good with the *husmanskost* – that means nice, everyday country food. I will be able to show to you some of my favoured Swedish dishes. That is good plan?"

"That's a very good plan," Star assured him happily. "I can't wait!"

For the next hour, the two of them, along with Tank, sampled a variety of Swedish delicacies, from *tunnbröd,* a thin, white crispbread, to *strömming,* or Baltic herring. The restaurant staff was attentive, bringing out course after course and refilling their glasses before the diners could notice they were empty. But they left them alone other than that, allowing them to relax and have a nice time chatting and laughing together. Sven's English was good enough that the language barrier rarely got in the way, and when it did, Tank translated.

The more time Star spent with Sven, the nicer she found him. The two of them talked about anything and everything – music, the weirdness of sudden fame, their childhoods, and much more. Star even found herself telling Sven about her family's disappearance. He listened sympathetically, then shyly suggested that she try writing a song about the experience.

Star was startled at the suggestion. "Wow, I never thought about that," she said. "How would I work something like that into a song?"

Sven shrugged. "Anything you like, it can become a song," he said. "Any idea, any – what is the word in English? Ah, feeling – emotion? All it is needed to be is real."

"I guess." Star took a sip of water. "But I'm still way new to this whole songwriting thing. I wouldn't even know where to start, you know?"

"I would be happy to help," Sven said. "I think it would be very much fun to try to be writing a song with you, Star."

"That would be excellent! Thanks, Sven."

Star smiled at him. Talking with Sven was so comfortable;

it was almost as if they'd known each other a lot longer than they really had. For a moment the PopTV rumour floated through her mind.

But she quickly shook off the thought. Her friendship with Sven wasn't like that – she was totally loyal to her sort-of boyfriend back home, Aaron Bickford. Still, she was glad she'd had the chance to get to know Sven better. Despite coming from different countries and speaking different languages, the two of them had a lot in common.

All too soon Star noticed Tank glancing at his watch. "Oh no, is it time to leave already?" she asked.

"Afraid so," Tank said, pushing back his chair. "We don't want to be late for Lukas Lukas."

Sven looked slightly alarmed. "Ah, no!" he said. "You do not want to be late for meeting with him. Lukas Lukas, he is famous here in Sweden for bad tempers about late meetings. You should go now. But I will see you tomorrow evening at the concert – or maybe before?" He gazed hopefully at Star. "If it agrees with your schedule, we could perhaps have lunch again tomorrow? And perhaps this time, we can try to write a new song, the two of us together."

"That sounds awesome!" Star said. "I'll check with my manager and let you know, okay?"

Outside the restaurant she found that a crowd had gathered while they ate. The local police had already set up barricades and were keeping eager fans and pushy photographers behind them, leaving a narrow pathway between the restaurant door and the limo parked at the curb. Star realized that Tank must have noticed the crowd gathering during one of the times he'd wandered away from the table, and called the police without her or Sven noticing.

"No time for autographs," Tank reminded her in a whisper. "Just wave and smile, and let's get out of here before we're late for Lukas."

Star nodded, took a deep breath, and stepped through the door. The crowd swelled forward, and it was all the police officers could do to hold them back.

"Hello, everyone!" Star cried, waving and smiling as Tank hustled her past the screaming crowd towards the waiting limo. "Hello! And thank you!"

Three

"And your parents and young brother. How did you feel after their so tragic disappearance? Please, tell me everything."

Star blinked, a little taken aback by the direct question. She was sitting on a zebra-print beanbag chair in Lukas Lukas's private office with the director looking down at her from behind a polished Lucite desk. Everything in the office was black, white, or transparent, from the rug to the telephone to the framed photos on the walls. The director himself was much more colourfully dressed in a vibrant red sweater and baggy plaid trousers. His shaggy black hair stood up in every direction, while his droopy dark eyes peered out from beneath the single black eyebrow that seemed to crawl across his face like a giant caterpillar.

"Erm – I was upset, of course," Star said uncertainly, her hand creeping up to touch the star pendant – a special gift from her parents – that she always wore around her neck.

She took a deep breath as the director waited silently for her to go on. "But I knew they wouldn't want me to give up on them. And I haven't. I know I'll find them again someday – I just wish it could happen soon. I miss them."

Lukas Lukas stared back at her blandly. "Good, good." He jotted a few notes on the pad in front of him. "We shall talk more about that later. First, though, I want you to tell me about the stories I am hearing about you and our own young Sven."

Star glanced quickly at Mike, who was sitting quietly in a chair near the door. Before entering the director's office, he had reminded Star to let him know if she needed any help. Lukas Lukas had graciously agreed that Star's manager could sit in on the interview, but the director seemed vaguely irritated whenever Mike said anything or even moved too abruptly in his seat. Star decided she could handle this question too on her own.

"Those rumours are just that – rumours," she said firmly. "Sven is a great person, but we're just friends."

"Good, good," Lukas Lukas murmured again in accented English. "This means you have a boyfriend back in America? Someone special, *ja*?"

Star gulped, startled. "Er – huh?" she said. "A boyfriend? No, not really."

"Not really, not really, not really," Lukas Lukas chanted. "But really — who is he? Please, will you tell me this boy's name, my dear? It is very important that I know." He leaned forward, his droopy jowls rearranging themselves into a wistful sort of smile. "I will not tell the media vultures, you have my word on that, my dear."

"Oh! I wasn't worried about . . . er . . . that is . . ." Star stammered. She was rarely at a loss for words, but something about Lukas Lukas's blunt questions and inquisitive stare confused her. "I mean, there is a boy — his name is Aaron," she blurted out. "But we're not exactly boyfriend-girlfriend or anything. I mean, I hardly ever get to see him. We e-mail each other a lot, though." She felt her cheeks turn red and wondered what it was about Lukas Lukas that made it impossible to evade his questions. Star had done hundreds of interviews over the past two years. But even the slickest professional journalist had never been able to pry Aaron's existence out of her.

"Perfect." Lukas Lukas seemed satisfied with her answer. After jotting another note, he leaned back in his chair and locked his hands behind his head, which made his hair stand up more wildly than ever. "Now, we will talk about the video. What is your vision for this song, my dear?"

Star hid a smile. So far, the director was certainly living up to his reputation for being eccentric. But Star didn't mind. Despite the occasional uncomfortable question, she found Lukas Lukas interesting and oddly likable.

"Well, the song is called 'Blast From the Past'," she said. "It's supposed to be the next single from my album. It's about, like, the history of popular music and stuff."

"Yes, yes, of course." Lukas Lukas clapped his hands. "It is a wonderful song. I was listening to it just before your arrival. I am filled with ideas – but now that I have met you, my dear, I have so many more! For one thing, you must please agree that your delightful pooch can play a role?"

Star glanced down at Dudley, who was napping on a second beanbag chair nearby. The little dog had come along with Mike to the director's studio, and at first they had planned to leave him in the car with Tank. But Lukas Lukas had been waiting for them on the street outside the studio, and as soon as he spotted the little pug he had insisted they bring him along to the meeting. He'd even ordered an assistant to bring Dudley a snack.

"Cool," Star said. "Dudley would love to be in a video!" She grinned at Lukas Lukas, who grinned back with delight.

"Stupendous!" the director said, clapping his hands again. "My cameramen tell me they have much good footage already. And of course, they will continue to accompany you, with Mr Mosley's gracious assent."

He bowed his head gallantly towards Mike, who nodded back. "Of course," Mike said. "They're welcome to come along as long as necessary."

"Good, good, good. But that will not be enough." Lukas Lukas stood up and paced back and forth behind his desk. "We will need additional footage." He stopped and turned abruptly to face Star. "Can you be available tomorrow afternoon? We'll need to hold auditions then – your background dancers will be needed, of course, but also many other parts. You would like to have input in that?"

"Oh, yes!" Star said. "That sounds really fun!"

Lukas Lukas seemed pleased with her answer. "And the following day I will spend planning, and the day after that we will do the shooting," he went on. "That way you will not have to think of it again once you leave Sweden. I will take care of everything else."

"Um . . ." Star glanced helplessly towards Mike. She had no idea what was on her schedule for the next few days.

"Well, let's see here." Mike was already pulling a notebook

out of his pocket. He flipped through it quickly. "Yes, I think I can move some things around. How about if I have her back here tomorrow around this same time? And I'll let the dancers know to keep the next day all clear."

This time Lukas Lukas didn't seem bothered at all by Mike's input. In fact, he seemed thrilled. "Marvellous!" he cried. "It is a date, then. Now, if you'll excuse me, I have to see a man about a herring."

Without another word he dashed out the door. A moment later an assistant appeared to show them out. They found Tank waiting in the lobby, which was decorated like a beach resort, with colourful umbrellas, teak deck chairs, and a large pile of sand in the corner beyond the reception desk, which was itself disguised as a hot dog stand.

"How was it?" Tank asked, pushing himself up from the lounge chair where he'd been sitting.

"Turns out the stories didn't do him justice," Mike replied quietly, rubbing his mustache and glancing over his shoulder as if fearing the eccentric director might suddenly pop up behind him. "He's an odd duck, that's for sure."

Star giggled. "I liked him," she said. "He's, like, totally creative, you know? I can already tell he doesn't let anything stand in the way when he has an idea. Or a question," she added, remembering the slightly uncomfortable queries about her family and Aaron.

Mike shot her a sharp glance. "Very perceptive," he said. "Come to think of it, you two should get on well together – you're both a little nuts."

Star giggled, and Tank grinned. "I'll take Dudley for a quick walk and then go get the car," he said, pulling the pug's leash out of his pocket. "Give me five minutes."

As Tank and Dudley disappeared through the front door and Mike wandered off in search of the restroom, Star sat down in a striped canvas beach chair. The chair tipped her back slightly, and she found herself staring up at the ceiling, where several fake gulls were circling on a ceiling fan. She grinned, impressed with Lukas Lukas's attention to detail and offbeat sense of humour. What would the tryouts for the video be like? She was glad the director had invited her to attend, even though she knew it would mean rushing to fit in all the other things she was scheduled to do.

That was when she belatedly remembered her impulsive invitation to fly her friends over for a visit. She gulped, realizing that her schedule for the next few days didn't look quite as easy and open as when she'd dashed off that e-mail the night before. That morning after breakfast, she had checked her e-mail and found a brief reply from Missy promising to check with her parents and the other invitees and write back as soon as possible. Since then, Star had heard nothing more.

Maybe I should wait until I hear back from her, she thought. *If it turns out they can't make it, I don't want to get Mike all worked up for nothing. . . .*

Almost before the thought was completed, she was shaking her head. She knew she wouldn't feel right doing that. Especially not now. During the tour's recent stop in Rome, Star had sneaked away without Mike's permission, flying all the way to America to check out a new clue in the search for her missing family. Mike had forgiven her and said no more about it since then, but Star still felt terrible about the whole incident. She had promised herself never to deceive Mike again, and she planned to keep that vow.

Soon Mike returned from the bathroom. "Tank back yet?" he asked.

"No," Star said. "But listen – there's something I forgot to tell you earlier."

Speaking fast before she lost her nerve, she spilled the whole story. Mike listened quietly, rubbing his chin.

"I see," he said when she finished, sounding slightly exasperated. "You know, it would probably be better to discuss this sort of thing with me first."

"Sorry," Star said contritely. "It was sort of an impulse. I meant to tell you this morning, but with the stuff about Sven and everything, I guess I forgot." She bit her lip. "If you think it's a bad idea, I can call Missy and tell her to forget it."

Mike's expression softened. "No need for that," he said. "Now that we have this video business to deal with, do you think you can still handle everything, even with your friends here?"

Star's eyes widened as she realized that Mike wasn't saying no to the plan after all. "Sure!" she said excitedly. "I swear, you can count on me." She took a deep breath. "So does that mean it's okay if they come? If their parents and everyone say it's okay, I mean?"

Mike shrugged. "Don't see why not," he replied gruffly. "You know what Lola's always saying about all work and no play. And for once she's right. You've been working hard, and you deserve a little fun if anyone does." His face crinkled into a smile. "If their folks all clear the trip, I'll make the arrangements."

"Cool!" Star jumped up and down gleefully. "Thanks, Mike, you're totally awesome!" Suddenly she remembered one detail she'd forgotten to mention. "Oh, um, I also sort of told them I'd pay for everything if they came," she admitted. "I hope that's okay – I guess it could get expensive to fly four or five people over here and everything."

Mike chuckled. "Darlin', with the way your new album has been selling, you could fly the whole darn town of New Limpet over here without the accountants even noticing it. Not that I'm suggestin' that, of course," he added hurriedly.

Star giggled. "Don't worry," she said. "Just these guys will be enough for now." She sighed. "I just wish I could convince Nans to fly over for a visit. But she hates planes."

"I know," Mike said kindly. "But you'll see her soon when you fly home during your break." He checked his watch. "I wonder what's keeping Tank? We have a lot to do if we're going to fit everything in this week."

Before Star could answer, she heard the jingle of the bell outside the lobby door. "Maybe that's him now," she said, glancing towards the entrance.

But instead of Tank, she saw a different familiar face entering the studio lobby. "Jade!" Star gasped in surprise.

Jade looked startled too. But she quickly regained her composure and her usual slightly bored expression. "Hey," she said. "How's it going?"

"Fine." Star was relieved to see that Jade's rude, obnoxious manager, Stan Starkey, didn't appear to be with her. Instead Starkey's assistant, a tense young woman named Manda Smith, followed her into the studio along with several bodyguards.

Mike nodded politely to the bodyguards, then to the assistant. "Howdy, Manda," he said. "Nice to see you again."

The woman looked slightly suspicious, but returned his smile. "Yes, great," she said, stepping towards him. "Listen, Mosley, as long as you're here, I need to ask you about a couple of things. . . ."

As the two adults chatted Star stepped closer to Jade, who was leaning against a folded-up beach umbrella. "So you're going to do a video with Lukas Lukas too, huh?" Star said.

"Looks that way," Jade replied. "So what's he like? I heard he's all kinds of strange."

Star giggled. "Does the word megabiggaweirdo mean anything to you?"

Jade raised an eyebrow. "Seriously?"

"So serious." Star crossed her heart. "But he's cool. I think you'll like him – he's super-creative, and he really listened to what I had to say. Not all adults do that, you know?"

Jade nodded, her expression a little friendlier. "That's cool," she said. "Weird I can handle, as long as the guy's not a jerk or something, you know? I just wasn't sure what this Lukas dude is all about. I don't really know that much about the other stuff he's done."

"Really? I guess I didn't either until Mike told me about him," Star said. "So was it the video he did for Eddie Urbane that made you want to work with him?"

Jade shrugged and examined her manicured fingernails. "Hey, *you're* doing a video with him, right?"

Star wrinkled her forehead, not quite understanding the sudden sarcasm in Jade's voice. "What do you mean?"

"I mean if Star Calloway does it, it has to be the thing to do – at least in The World According to Stan." Jade met her eyes briefly, then looked away. "He's totally obsessed with your career, haven't you noticed?" She played with the fringe of the folded beach umbrella. "I sure have. You're practically all he ever talks about. Star did this, Star won that, blah blah Star blah . . ."

"For real?" Star felt more than a little uncomfortable. All of a sudden Jade was looking downright angry. Was she mad at Starkey, or Star, or both?

Just then Mike called her name from over near the door,

where he was standing with Manda. "Car's here," he said when Star looked over.

"Guess I've got to go," Star told Jade apologetically. "Listen, um . . ." She still wasn't sure what to say about what Jade had just told her. "Good luck with Lukas Lukas," she said instead. "I'm sure you'll have fun with him."

"Thanks. See you."

Star headed out to the limo with Mike and climbed in. Soon Tank was steering through the picturesque streets of Stockholm toward their next appointment.

"Well, that was an interesting coincidence," Mike commented as he leaned back against the limo's leather seat.

"What's that?" Tank asked.

"We ran into Jade and a few of her people," Star told him. She glanced over at Mike. "Hey, what did that Manda woman want to ask you about, anyway?"

Mike stroked his mustache. "Seems Starkey doesn't teach her much about the business," he said rather cryptically.

When he didn't elaborate, Star decided that meant he didn't want to talk about it. She shrugged and let it drop.

"Anyway," she said, "Jade said something a little weird to me just now. She said Stan Starkey is obsessed with my career. He wants her to do everything I do, like work with Lukas Lukas and stuff."

"Bizarre," Tank commented, glancing at Star and Mike in the rearview mirror. "Can't be healthy being so interested in someone else's career."

"Probably no picnic for poor Jade, either," Mike added. "She's doing awfully well for her stage of the game. It's one thing to follow someone's example or whatnot – everyone does that – but just out and out comparing her to someone who's already more established like you are is about as useful as toenail polish on a warthog."

Star nodded slowly, thinking about what Mike was saying. What would it be like to have a manager who thought some other performer was better than you, who was never satisfied with what you could provide? She couldn't even imagine it; Mike and the rest of her crew never let her think she had anything to prove to anyone.

Of course, they don't let me think I'm better than anyone else either, she thought fondly. *If I ever started to get a big head about this whole deal, they'd be sure to let me know it! It's too bad Jade doesn't seem to have anyone like that on her team – not from what I can tell, anyhow.*

"I guess I should've realized Jade's team was kind of messed up after the way they spread the secret about my family," Star commented. She gasped, realizing what she had just said. "Oh! You don't think they could be behind this latest rumour about me and Sven, do you?"

"Doubt it," Mike said. "The last thing Starkey would want is more publicity for you, good or bad – think he learned his lesson 'bout that the last time around."

In the front seat, Tank nodded. "Mike's right," he said. "My money's still on Urbane. This seems more up his alley."

Just then Mike's phone rang. He fished it out of his pocket and flipped it open.

"Mosley here," he said. "Oh, hi, Tricia. What's up?" He listened for a moment, nodding even though Tricia couldn't see him.

"What was that about?" Star asked when he hung up.

Mike smiled. "Seems there's a message for you on the answering service back at the hotel," he said. "A certain Miss Takamori called to let you know that she'll be available to visit this week, along with a few other young Americans of your acquaintance."

Star gasped. "Really? They're coming?" Her heart leaped with joy, making her realize that she'd missed her friends even more than she'd thought. "That's so awesome! I can't wait to see them! I want to take them for a real Swedish smorgasbord like the one we had our first night here, and maybe meet Sven so he can show us around a little, and . . ."

"Hold your horses." Mike raised one hand in caution. "Now, just because your friends are coming, you can't go rushing off and forget about everything else. You have a lot of stuff to do over the next few days."

"Don't worry about a thing. I'll totally do all of it, I swear." Star was so excited she could barely sit still. She felt like standing up and leaping through the sunroof of the limo to dance on the roof just to express her happiness. Instead, she settled for a big grin and a shiver of anticipation. "This is going to be great!"

Four

The next morning Star's eyes were barely open when she remembered the news about her friends and bounced out of bed, startling the still-sleeping Dudley so much that he tumbled off the edge of the bed onto the rug. She raced down the stairs in her nightgown, not even bothering to pull on a robe.

"Well?" she demanded of Mike, who was sitting alone at the dining table sipping coffee and reading the newspaper.

He glanced up at her. "Well what?" he asked, straight-faced. When Star growled playfully at him, he broke into a grin. "Just kiddin', sweetheart. Everything's all set. Your friends will be here first thing tomorrow morning. I managed to get them booked on an overnight nonstop from Philly — even found enough seats for them in first class, just like you requested."

"Yahoo!" Star clapped her hands and did a little leap-kick movement from one of her dance routines, almost knocking over a lamp. "Thanks, Mike – you're the best! Better than the best!"

Mike chuckled. "Thanks." Then his face grew serious again. "But I'm afraid all the news isn't good this morning. Take a look."

He pushed the newspaper across the table. Star stepped forward and saw that it was an English-language European newspaper. It was open to the entertainment section, and a huge headline screamed STAR AND SVEN: HOT STUFF UP NORTH!

"Yikes," she said, leaning down to pat Dudley, who had just made it downstairs. "Guess this means those rumours haven't died down yet."

"Not hardly," Mike said grimly. "In fact, they seem to be taking hold and expanding like blisters. Tricia called a little while ago to say that some sources are actually claimin' that you and Sven snuck off and got hitched!"

"No way! You mean married?" Star laughed. "That's so crazy!"

Mike sighed. "See for yourself."

He tossed her another newspaper, this one a tabloid based in London. Star sat down and read the story, which went into breathless detail about the imaginary nuptials, comparing Star and Sven to Romeo and Juliet. At first Star was amused by the whole thing. But towards the end the article went on to speculate that Sven was only after Star for her fame, and to predict that the new marriage would last only as long as it took for Sven's international music career to take off.

As she finished the article Tank entered from the direction of the kitchen holding a steaming cup of coffee. "Want some breakfast, Star-baby?" he asked. "Mags is in there making pancakes."

"No, thanks," Star murmured. "I'm not hungry all of a sudden." She looked up at Mike. "This article makes Sven sound like some kind of shallow jerk," she said. "He's not really like that at all!"

"I know that, and you know that," Mike replied sombrely. "But as you know, a lot of people believe whatever they read in the newspaper or see on TV."

Star flipped through the pile of newspapers, all of which were open to news about her. She came to one that was written in Swedish, so she couldn't read the headlines, but she noticed a picture of a group of teenagers standing around a bonfire. Several of the teens in the photo were wearing Star Calloway concert T-shirts.

"What are they doing?" she asked, confused.

Tank leaned over her shoulder to see. "Yowza," he said. "The caption says those are some of your local fan club members, Star. They're burning their Sven CDs because they think he's using you."

Star gasped. "You're kidding!" she cried in horror. "That's awful!"

She wasn't feeling the least bit amused by the stories anymore. Even though she was getting used to having nutty things written about her, she hated to think that Sven's promising new career might be hurt or even ruined because of her.

"We've got to do something," she declared, flipping to the next newspaper, an American one that featured a full-colour artist's rendition of what Star and Sven's secret wedding might have looked like. "Maybe hold a press conference, or release a statement or something . . . Hey, check this out."

On the page below the drawing of her and Sven, she pointed to a smaller photo of Eddie Urbane. A short blurb beneath the picture stated that the young star had been spotted arriving in Tibet three days earlier, and had been meditating on a mountaintop there ever since with the help of his latest girlfriend, new age guru Xandra Om.

Mike and Tank leaned over to see. "Hmm, looks like Urbane ditched his American tour yet again," Mike commented.

Star nodded. Eddie's tour had started at about the same

time as hers, but he had managed to cancel or postpone more shows than he'd actually performed so far. First he had flown off to Italy to be with his then-girlfriend, an Italian supermodel. Now it seemed he had followed his latest love all the way to Tibet.

"You know what this means, don't you?" Tank pointed to a line in the article. "Says here the place where Urbane and Om are has no phones or other modern conveniences. It doesn't even get a mobile phone service – total isolation. If they've been there for the past three days . . ."

"That means he couldn't be behind the new rumours," Star finished, realizing what Tank was getting at. "That's weird. So then where did those stories come from? I mean, we didn't plant them, obviously. And I'm positive that Sven didn't either – he's just not that kind of person. And you know his manager, right?"

"Right," Mike said. "He's not the type to pull something like this either."

He rubbed his chin thoughtfully. Before he could say anything else, the villa door swung open and Tricia raced in, clutching her usual manila folder to the breast of her stylish black suit.

"Morning, all!" she cried loudly. "Isn't it a fabulous day?

The sun is shining, the bees are buzzing . . . and everyone in the world is talking about our own little Star here!"

She rushed over and pinched one of Star's cheeks. Then she tossed her folder onto the table, almost upsetting Tank's coffee cup. He caught it just in time to keep it from spilling all over the pile of newspapers.

"Is that coffee?" Tricia said brightly. "I wouldn't mind a cup. I take it with no milk, three sugars. Oh, and a touch of fresh nutmeg if you've got it."

Tank and Mike exchanged a glance. Mike looked slightly annoyed, but Tank seemed amused.

"I'll get right on that," he said, standing up. "Anyone else? Star?"

"No, thanks," Star replied, still staring at the picture of Eddie. If he wasn't spreading the crazy rumours about her, then who was?

"We were just looking over the news stories," Mike told Tricia as Tank disappeared into the kitchen. "They're rather – er – ubiquitous this morning."

Tricia yanked out a chair and sat down, flipping open her folder and scrabbling through the clippings inside. "I know, isn't it great?" she exclaimed cheerfully. "You can't buy publicity like this!"

Star frowned, surprised that Tricia seemed so happy about it. "But none of these stories are true," she said. "Sven and I aren't married. We're not even, like, dating or whatever. And I'm afraid all these crazy rumours might hurt him or his career."

Tricia smiled. "Aren't you sweet?" she cooed. "But seriously, darling, Sven should thank you if anything. Just remember the saying – any publicity is good publicity."

She immediately turned to Mike and started chattering at him about some upcoming interviews. Star gazed at the publicist, not much liking the suspicious new thoughts forming in her mind.

Could it be? she wondered uneasily. *Could Tricia be planting the stories about Sven just to keep me on the front pages?*

Star trusted her core team completely. Despite Lola's occasional over-enthusiastic statements to the press, she knew that none of them would ever purposely hurt her in any way. But she had learned that not everyone was so reliable. Not long before the start of the tour Mike had hired a gopher named Vernon who had turned out to be working for Eddie Urbane. With Vernon's help Eddie had almost sabotaged Star's tour. Could Tricia be planting the stories without admitting it just to drum up more publicity for Star and make her own job easier? Worse yet, could she be working for Eddie just like Vernon?

As Star was thinking, there was a loud buzz, like a swarm of angry bees. She looked around, wondering what was making the weird noise.

Tank had just entered with Tricia's coffee. "That's the phone," he said, noticing Star's confusion. "I'll get it." He hurried over and grabbed the receiver of the sleek, modern telephone in the seating area nearby. "Hello?"

Star was still looking at him. She saw his broad face break into a grin.

"Well, hello there," he said. "Sure, we'll accept the charges, operator."

"Who is it?" Mike asked.

Tank tossed the cordless receiver to Star. "It's for her."

A little surprised, Star lifted the phone to her ear. "Hello?"

"Hey! It's me!" a very familiar voice, only slightly altered by the international phone lines, said into her ear.

Star gasped. "Missy!" she shrieked. "Is that really you?"

"Of course," Missy replied from the other end of the line. "Listen, I'm sorry about calling long distance and reversing the charges and stuff. But my parents would kill me if a call to Sweden showed up on their next bill."

"That's cool, I totally don't mind," Star said. "But why are you calling now? We're going to see each other in, like, twenty-four hours, right?" Suddenly a terrible thought struck her. "Wait, you're still coming, aren't you? Please say you're still coming!"

"Totally!" Missy answered right away. "But that's sort of why I'm calling. Someone else might not be coming with me."

"I know, I know," Star said, perching on the arm of an angular beige couch. "You already told me in your e-mail that Trina's parents won't let her miss her orthodontist appointment, and—"

"No, that's not what I'm talking about," Missy interrupted. "Just listen for a second, okay? It's about Aaron."

Star's heart jumped, as it always did when she thought about Aaron Bickford. "Aaron?" she repeated, lowering her voice slightly so the adults in the room wouldn't hear. "What about him?"

She heard Missy's sigh through the phone. "Okay, PopTV and, like, every entertainment show in the U.S. is showing you hanging out with some total hottie from over there in Sweden. Sven something?"

"Yeah, I know. Sven's my opening act while I'm here. The

rest is just some crazy story someone made up about us." Star didn't bother to go into further detail. She figured she could fill Missy in on the rest when she saw her in person.

"I figured it wasn't true," Missy said. "I mean, they're saying you and this Sven dude are, like, secretly married already. Totally crazy, right? But the trouble is, Aaron is acting kind of weird about the trip now."

"Huh?" Star blinked. "He doesn't actually believe the stories, does he?"

"He says he doesn't," Missy replied. "But you know how sensitive he is and stuff." She sighed loudly again. "I guess he thinks maybe there's some, like, kernel of truth or whatever that saying is, you know? Like, he doesn't actually believe you and this hot Swedish guy are married, but maybe he thinks there's *something* between you or they wouldn't write a story like that."

"Oh, but they would," Star said, her hand clenching the phone so tightly that her knuckles turned white. "They totally, totally would. You've got to convince him of that."

"I've been trying, and you know I won't give up until I'm boarding that plane tonight," Missy said. "But Aaron's being kind of stubborn about it, so I thought I should give you the 411 – just in case."

Star sighed. Part of her couldn't believe that Aaron was being so silly. Then again, maybe she *could* understand it. Even if he didn't believe the marriage rumours, Aaron could see from the photos that Star was hanging around with a good-looking, glamorous European singer. Was it really so surprising that he was willing to sadly, shyly bow out of this trip – and maybe Star's life? After all, despite e-mailing and texting each other regularly since Star's tour had begun, they still hadn't ever really admitted their true feelings to each other. . . .

For a moment she was tempted to call Aaron herself, to try to explain the rumours and let him know how much she wanted to see him. But she wasn't sure that was such a good idea. What if this was his way of letting her know he wasn't that interested in her after all? Besides, she tended to get a little tongue-tied around him. If she starting babbling nonsense over the international phone lines, she was likely to make the situation worse rather than better.

She was going to have to count on her best friend. "Do whatever you can," she told Missy tensely. "Please! You've got to make him understand that Sven and I are just friends, nothing more."

"I'll try. Oops, I think I hear Dad coming upstairs. I should probably go — easier than trying to explain what I'm doing talking to you on the phone. I don't want to make him mad after he and Mom just gave me permission to come over there. I'll see you tomorrow, okay?"

"See you then. 'Bye."

As the line went dead, Star hung up and wandered back toward the dining table. Tricia had left, Mike was over in the corner talking on his phone, and Mags had appeared with a pitcher of orange juice and a plate of pancakes.

"Ready for breakfast, Star?" she asked cheerfully.

Star sighed. "Not really," she muttered, flopping into a chair. "I'm not that hungry."

"Nonsense! As my late husband Colonel Nattle used to say every morning, breakfast is the most important meal of the day." Mags set the pancakes in front of Star and poured her a glass of orange juice. "Now help yourself, and we'll hit the books while you eat. We aren't going to have much time for studying this week, and even pop stars need to learn about the Great Depression."

"Okay," Star murmured, knowing better than to argue. With a soft sigh she accepted the juice and history books, doing her best to push all thoughts of Aaron out of her mind.

Five

Star was still feeling a little distracted when she reached the studio where she was meeting Sven. Thoughts of the Great Depression mixed in her head with the news stories and the conversation with Missy, all of it swirling together in a jumble of uneasy feelings.

Tank guided her past the customary cluster of fans and photographers who had turned out to meet her. Star waved and smiled as she always did, but her heart wasn't in it as much as usual.

Sven was waiting just inside the door in a long, brightly lit hallway lined with doors and decorated with framed gold records. At the sight of his smiling face Star instantly felt a little bit better.

"Hi!" she greeted him happily.

Then she gulped, wondering if she was a little *too* happy to see him. *What if Aaron is right?* she thought. *What if I'm*

getting a little crush on Sven without even realizing it? Maybe he's right to be worried.

"Hej, Star." Sven returned her greeting, not seeming to notice her consternation. "I am so happy you are here."

He stepped forward, clearly expecting a friendly hug. Star quickly sidestepped, sticking out her hand.

"Me too," she said briskly, grabbing his hand and pumping it up and down several times before dropping it again. "Hey, let's head inside and get started on that lunch you promised, okay? I'm starved."

That much was true. At Mags's urging, she had nibbled at a pancake or two at breakfast, but her stomach had been churning too much at the newest rumours for her to eat much. Now, though, it was grumbling and complaining, and Star knew she'd better eat a couple of good meals before her concert that evening or she was likely to poop out halfway through the first dance number.

Sven looked troubled. "Are you unhappy with me, Star?" he asked. "You seem as if you are angry. Is it about the rumours? I have tried my best to explain to the reporters that the stories they are not true, but . . ."

"No, no," Star said hastily, realizing that her odd behaviour was causing even Tank to give her a strange look. "It's totally fine. I understand. I – I guess I'm just a little distracted. I'm supposed to go watch the tryouts for my video after this, and I was just wondering what that would be like."

Sven looked relieved. Seeming satisfied with her explanation, he greeted Tank politely in Swedish and then led them both into the studio. It was a low-ceilinged, green-painted room with recording equipment lining most of the walls. In the centre of the room stood a grand piano, and several guitars were lying on a table nearby. A buffet-style lunch was laid out on a second table near the entrance, featuring Swedish foods such as meatballs, brown beans, crispbread, and crayfish.

"Wow, this looks great!" Star stepped over to the table and surveyed the food.

"Absolutely," Tank agreed. "Think I'll just help myself to a plate and take it out to the waiting room if you kids don't mind." He gestured to a large plateglass window in one wall. Through it Star could see a comfortable-looking room filled with upholstered furniture and potted plants.

"You don't have to go, Tank," she said quickly, suddenly a little nervous at the idea of being alone with Sven. "You can stay here with us if you want."

Tank smiled. "Thanks, Star-baby," he said. "But I have

some contracts to read for Mike and some other work to do. Besides, I'll just be in the way of your songwriting and such."

Star smiled back weakly. Tank had been with her team so long that it sometimes seemed as if he could read her mind. Obviously this wasn't one of those times.

"Okay," she said. "Um, let's eat!"

Soon Tank was gone, and she and Sven pulled up chairs and sat down across from each other to eat.

"This food is really good," Star said after a moment, still feeling awkward about being there with Sven. If Aaron could see them now, would he think they were on a date? Would he be right?

Sven swallowed a mouthful of herring and nodded. "This food company – what is the word in English? When people bring you food?"

"Uh – waiters?" Star guessed.

"No, no, not like that." Sven shook his head, looking slightly frustrated. "It is when they prepare the food, and bring it to you – at your home, or wherever."

"Delivery? Like from a restaurant?" Star guessed.

"Not a restaurant," Sven said. "For special events and such."

"Oh! You mean catering!" Star grinned. "You mean you had the lunch catered. Right?"

"Yes!" Sven threw his head back. "Thank you! I could not recall the English word."

Star giggled. Sven seemed so happy about finding the answer. That was one of the things she had liked about him right away – he was enthusiastic about all sorts of strange things, just like she was.

"I will have to be sure to remember it next time, in case you are not around to help me," Sven went on with a grin. He grabbed one of the guitars from the other table and strummed a chord. "Perhaps I need to write a song about it." He cleared his throat, rolled his eyes to the ceiling, and sang dramatically, "Catering, catering, I love you so . . . Catering, catering, please please don't go-o-o-o!"

Soon his silly lyrics had Star laughing so hard she dropped her fork. After that it was much easier to put her troubles out of her mind and enjoy herself. Sven was a lot of fun, and she didn't want to waste this chance to get to know him better.

After he finished his catering song, Sven took a few more bites of his lunch. Then he sat back with the guitar and strummed a few chords.

"Hey, that last riff sounded good," Star said. "Did you just come up with that?"

Sven nodded. "I like to play with different sounds – to try

all kinds of things and see what sounds good and right to me. That is the way most of my songs start."

"Cool." Star hummed the riff. "That one sounds like a chorus. All it needs is a cool lyric – la LA la la la la la. Hmm. How about, 'My lunch is so delicious'?"

Sven grinned. "Not bad," he said. "What about, 'This herring is so tasty'?"

"No, no, no," Star said. She pushed herself back from the table and stood up. "This herring is delicious!" she sang out, with one hand on her chest and the other waving dramatically.

"Sounds great," Sven said, laughing. "Then again, almost any lyric sounds great when you sing it. Why do you not try singing my catering song? It could be a masterpiece. We could make it a number-one hit! Come on, you know we can – together we can do it!"

"That's it!" Star cried.

"What's it?" Sven looked confused.

Star cleared her throat. "Together we can do it," she sang. "Together we can try."

"We can make it happen," Sven sang, picking up her lead. He strummed a new chord on the guitar. "Together . . . Er, okay, I have lost it."

Star smiled. "Yeah, me too," she said. "But that sounded pretty good, didn't it?" Leaning against the edge of the table, she hummed the tune again. "Wait, maybe that second line should change. What about something like, 'We have to take a chance'?"

Sven nodded. "That's good," he said, picking out the melody as he spoke. "Or what about, 'We have to make it real'?"

"I love it!" Star waggled her fingers at the guitar. "Play the opening riff again, and let's take it from the top . . ."

Before long they had sketched out a chorus and several verses of their new song. Sven picked out the accompanying chords on the guitar as they went along, and they even worked out a few harmony parts.

"Wow," Star said after they ran through the whole thing. "I hate to brag, but that really sounded pretty good!"

"It is not bragging, really," Sven told her. "It is something we have created from our minds, and it is important for us to be proud. Otherwise what is the reason for writing music at all?"

"Good point." Sven was so smart about certain things – he almost made writing songs seem easy. "It's so weird," Star commented. "Just, like, half an hour ago, our song didn't even exist. Now it does!" She laughed, slightly embarrassed. "I guess that sounds dumb, doesn't it?"

"Not at all," Sven assured her. "I know just what you mean."

Star smiled at him. One other thing had changed in the past half hour: She and Sven had become much closer. Writing a song together was a surprisingly intimate process. The two of them had shared thoughts and ideas and feelings, and the process had advanced their relationship in a way that might have taken weeks or months of ordinary socializing.

But Star was beginning to realize that such intimacy didn't have to mean romance. She was more certain than ever that Sven was just a friend. That was all – and that was enough.

I just wish Aaron knew that, she thought, glancing worriedly at the clock on the studio wall. Her friends would be heading to the airport in a matter of hours. If Missy was going to change Aaron's mind about staying home, she had to do it quickly.

All too soon, Tank poked his head into the room. "Time to start winding things up," he told them. "Star, we need to leave for those auditions in about ten minutes."

Star nodded. "Be right there, Tank." She shot Sven an

apologetic glance. "Sorry I have to go so soon. This was really fun; I wish we could keep going."

"I understand," Sven said. "It is okay. Our song is nearly finished, anyway. I can work out the last few lines if you like, then show you this evening after the concert if you are not too tired."

"That would be great!" This time Star didn't feel awkward at all about reaching out and giving him a hug. "Thanks, Sven. See you later."

"Hey, Star! We were just wondering if you were coming."

Star turned and saw Rachel and Erin Maxwell waving at her from across the warm-up room at Lukas Lukas's studio. Several other dancers from the tour were nearby, stretching or chatting or sipping water. They all added their own waves and smiles of greeting.

"Hi, guys," Star replied with a smile for all of them. She wandered over to Rachel and Erin, happy to have a few minutes to hang out with them. "So, I hope you all don't mind turning out for this," she said. "I know it was supposed to be an afternoon off."

Erin shrugged. "No biggie," she said, stretching down to touch her toes with the heels of her hands. "We're happy to have the chance to work with Lukas Lukas."

Rachel shoved her twin playfully. "You mean you're happy to have the chance to get your face in a video," she teased.

Star giggled as Erin shoved her sister back. "Okay, no fighting, you two," she joked. "Otherwise I'll make sure Lukas puts you both way in the back so nobody will be able to see you."

"You wouldn't dare!" Rachel gasped in mock horror.

Erin shoved her again. "Hush," she said. "Don't talk back to the teacher."

"Now, what did I just tell you about fighting?" Star waggled her finger. "It's all fun and games until someone loses a tooth."

Rachel looked confused. "Wait, I thought that saying was 'It's all fun and games until someone loses an eye'?"

Star bit her lip, realizing what she'd said. The saying she'd used was her own invention; she and Missy had come up with it years and years ago after Missy had lost one of her baby teeth playing soccer in Star's backyard. Ever since then the two of them and several of their friends had used it jokingly whenever an opportunity presented itself.

"Oops," Star said, a little embarrassed. Why would she expect Rachel and Erin to get her inside joke with her old friends? After all, she'd only known them for a couple of months. "Guess you're right."

Suddenly she wasn't really in the mood for fooling around anymore. Homesickness filled her from head to toe, making her wish that her friends from home were already there. Rachel and Erin and the other dancers were great, and so was Sven, but they just weren't the same.

"Excuse me," she said. "I've got to go check on something before we get started."

She hurried to the waiting room where she'd left her purse. Digging into it, she pulled out her handheld computer and turned it on. She held her breath as she opened her e-mail. Would there be a message from Missy?

There was. Star clicked on it, hoping for good news. But the text of Missy's message was brief: "Still working on it."

Six

"Pickle, my dear?" ~~Lukas~~ Lukas asked gallantly, holding out a small ceramic tray filled with a variety of slimy-looking items that bore no resemblance to anything Star would consider a pickle.

She wanted to wrinkle her nose at the sour smell wafting out of the pickle dish, but she forced herself to maintain a pleasant expression. "No, thank you," she said. "I had a big lunch."

"Fine, fine. More for me!" Lukas ~~Lukas~~ chuckled at his joke and popped a purplish bit of pickled something-or-other into his mouth.

Then he waved one hand above his head. "All right!" he called. "Send in the next person, if you please!"

Star leaned forward eagerly. She was really enjoying the video auditions. For the past half hour or so she had been sitting at a long folding table beside the director as performer after performer filed in to try out. Unlike much of the rest of

Lukas's studio, this room looked surprisingly ordinary; it was a large, airy, brightly lit room with a wooden floor and mirrors on the wall. Star's background dancers were taking turns dancing with each person auditioning, helping to test who could really handle the part.

A choreographer and a couple of Lukas's other people were also at the table with him and Star, and at the end of each tryout they either congratulated the dancer auditioning and asked him or her to wait outside until the next round, or merely thanked the person and said goodbye. Star felt a little sorry for the ones who were sent away, but most of them seemed to take it in their stride.

I guess it's like when I was just getting started and would audition for commercial parts or sing for different record company scouts and stuff, she thought. *Mike taught me early on that not every gig is a perfect fit for every artist. Also that I should listen to criticism but not take it too much to heart.*

Just then Mike returned from the hallway outside the tryout room, where he had spent the past half hour making calls on his mobile phone. He slid into the empty seat beside Star. The floor in front of the table was vacant except for several tour dancers who were waiting for the next person to enter.

"So what are we doing now?" Mike whispered.

Lukas Lukas heard him and leaned over to answer. "We now are looking for someone to play the part of the leading man," he explained. "That is the boy who will be Star's primary dance partner in several sequences – the Roaring Twenties scene, the fifties sock hop scene, and so forth. It is the most important role in the video aside from Star herself."

Star nodded, still impressed with the way the director was envisioning the video for her song. Lukas Lukas had explained that the fictional sequences they were filming in the studio would be interspersed with bits of the live concert footage his cameramen were shooting at her shows.

"This is going to be an awesome video!" she exclaimed, shivering slightly with excitement.

Lukas Lukas picked up another pickle between his thumb and forefinger, gazing at it thoughtfully. "Yes," he said. "But only if we can find the right person for this particular part. No one we have seen so far is even close to what we are looking for. The young man must be handsome, with a unique and unmistakable face that will be recognizable through all the various costume changes. He must be likable and sweet, charismatic but humble. Close to your age, but not too childish or immature or too short. It would be helpful if he were blond, to match with your own colouring. And of course he must also be an excellent and versatile dancer . . ."

Star couldn't help thinking about Sven. *He would be great for the part,* she thought. *Handsome, sweet, blond, a good dancer with a recognizable face – I bet he'd do it, too. It's almost like Lukas Lukas is describing him personally. It's perfect!*

But was it *too* perfect? She chewed on her lip, struck with sudden doubt. What if Lukas Lukas really *was* describing Sven? He obviously knew about the rumours – what if he was the one who had started them?

Everyone loves this kind of publicity – any kind of publicity, really! Tricia's words floated through Star's mind. Was it true? Was Lukas Lukas hoping to stir up some extra publicity for his own career by casting Star and her alleged love interest together in his latest masterpiece? And his cameramen were nearly the only approved photographers at the last concert – he easily could have provided the press with that mysterious backstage picture. . . .

Star sighed. These latest rumours were making her suspicious of everyone. She was pretty sure that Lukas Lukas wasn't that sort of person. But just in case, she decided to keep quiet about Sven. If her suspicions happened to be right, she didn't want to make things easier by playing into the director's plans. Besides, no matter who was behind the rumours, the last thing Aaron needed to hear at the moment was that Star's alleged new boyfriend would be starring as her leading man in her new video.

She was distracted from such thoughts as the next hopeful entered the room. He was a short, skinny man in his late twenties or early thirties, which made him close to a decade older than most of the other dancers who had auditioned so far. He had messy blond hair and a beaklike hooked nose, and he was wearing faded jeans, trainers, and a well-worn Star Calloway T-shirt.

"This is supposed to be your leading man?" Mike whispered in her ear.

Star shrugged. Beside her, Lukas Lukas was frowning. "What is this?" he cried, waving both hands above his head and almost sending his pickle dish flying. "Is this supposed to be a joke?" He added a flurry of words in his own language that Star didn't understand, but she noticed most of the Swedish-speakers in the room cringing.

"It is no joke, Mr Lukas," the young man said loudly in heavily accented English. "I am world's big Star Calloway fan, and here I am for her video to be a part."

The director rolled his eyes so dramatically that he

appeared to be looking up into his own bushy unibrow. "No, what you are doing is wasting my time and the time of this charming young lady." Lukas Lukas waved a hand towards Star, almost smacking her in the side of the head.

Star dodged just in time. She glanced at the young man, who looked so dejected at the director's words that Star couldn't help feeling sorry for him.

"It's okay," she told Lukas Lukas soothingly. "It won't hurt to let him try, right? He is sort of interesting-looking in an offbeat way – having someone like him in the video might be sort of cool."

She was mostly just trying to be nice – she didn't think for a second that Lukas Lukas would cast the scraggly-looking fan as her leading man – but the young man beamed at her as if she'd just promised him the world. "I thank you so much, Miss Calloway!" he cried with a gallant bow. "By the way, my name is called Lars. I am a dancer within my heart, though lessons and schooling I have not had so many. But I can learn well and fast, I believe. Already I know all of the steps to your video of the song 'Supernova', and as well the dances in video for 'Girl Talk'." He quickly shuffled his feet in what Star recognized as a vague approximation of the main dance steps in the latter video.

Star grinned. "So you're really a fan?" she said. "That's cool."

Lukas Lukas sighed loudly and waved his hand at the young man. "Fine," he growled. "Enough talking. Let us see what you can do, Lars. Proceed, please."

"Okay, your word is my command!" Lars exclaimed happily.

Two of the background dancers stepped forward into position, and the music for Star's song started. The dancers swung into motion on cue, but Lars did little more than hop around awkwardly between them. Within seconds it was clear that he had no idea what the steps were supposed to be – or if he did, he couldn't even come close to doing them.

Lukas Lukas let the tryout go on for about thirty seconds before waving his hand to cut the music. "Enough!" he exclaimed. "I have seen plenty. Now I think it is past time to move on." The other adults at the table, including Mike, nodded in agreement.

"What mean you, sir?" Lars cried breathlessly. "I am just feeling the music – the spirit, it is within me! I wish to interpret what Star's music it means to us who listen and love it!"

Star still felt sorry for Lars. He was so enthusiastic about her music, it seemed a shame to send him off without a word of encouragement. "Hold on," she said. "Mr Lukas, could we talk about this for a second?"

The director turned and stared at her in disbelief. "What are you saying to me, Star? You like this clown?"

"I don't know," Star said apologetically. She felt a little weird about speaking up for a guy she didn't even know in front of a room full of adults, but she just couldn't stand to see a true fan sent away without hope. "I just think we haven't given him enough of a chance," she explained. "He's got great energy, you know? Besides, wouldn't it be cool to have someone a little different in the video? Someone who doesn't look like everyone else in every other video on PopTV?"

She was a little surprised when Lukas Lukas nodded thoughtfully. "Perhaps you have a point, my dear," he said, running one hand through his wild hairdo. "After all, it is the rebels and the different who have often changed history throughout the rise of popular music. I suppose we should address that somehow. . . ."

Lars had stepped forward and was listening carefully. "This, does it mean I can in the video be?" he asked eagerly. "If so, I swear it that I will very hard work, and not let you down in any way!"

"We shall see," Lukas Lukas said sternly. "Away you go for now – we will call you in again for the next round, all right?"

"Wonderful!" Lars clapped his hands excitedly. "I thank you so very much – you especially, Star! You are my hero!"

He leaped towards the door, still clapping. Several of the adults chuckled, though Lukas Lukas still looked skeptical.

"Are you sure you want to consider this man for your video?" he asked Star.

"I think so." Star shrugged. "I mean, we're not having much luck finding a leading man anyway, right? So maybe we could split the part – let Lars be sort of comic relief or whatever in some of the scenes. One of my male tour dancers could fill in for the serious dance parts, and maybe some of the other not-quite-right actor-dancers we've seen could play other parts of the role. Know what I mean?"

Mike leaned forward. "Maybe we shouldn't second-guess Lukas's vision, sweetheart," he suggested, sounding slightly nervous.

Star guessed that he was worried she might offend the famously sensitive director. But far from looking upset, Lukas Lukas seemed rather intrigued by her idea.

"Yes, I suppose that might work – your image, it is quite playful, and your music it appeals to many facets of the world, just as the leading part could fragment into many facets . . . ," he mused aloud. He picked up a bit of pickle and stared at it as if it might hold the answers he needed. "And you are right that we have not found the right leading man I was envisioning. Perhaps this idea of yours, it is worth a try." Dropping the pickle abruptly, he turned to face Star with a big grin. "I will consider it," he said. "I thank you for your creative thoughts, my dear."

"You're totally welcome." Star smiled back, relieved at his reaction. "Thanks for listening."

About an hour later, just as the second round of dance auditions was getting started, Mike reminded Star that she had a concert to perform that evening. "We'd better get rollin'," he whispered. "You still need to eat and change clothes before we leave for the stadium."

"Oh," Star said. She was a little disappointed, even though she was looking forward to the concert. "I wish we could stay for the whole thing."

"Sorry," Mike said sympathetically. "Looks like these try-outs will be grinding on late into the evening."

After excusing themselves and promising Lukas Lukas that they would see him the day after tomorrow for the shoot, Star and Mike hurried out to the beach-themed lobby. Tank was waiting for them there, with Dudley on a leash at his feet.

"Hey there," he greeted them. "I was just going to come get you – thought you might've lost track of the time."

"Nope," Mike said with a smile. "But I practically had to hog-tie Star and drag her away from the auditions."

Tank chuckled, but then his expression turned serious again. "By the way, think I should warn you – we've got a little bit of a crowd waiting for us outside."

There was nothing unusual about that – all of Sweden seemed to know that Star was at Lukas's studio that day. But from the meaningful look Tank gave Mike, Star guessed there was more to it than that.

"What?" she demanded. "What is it, Tank? Please tell me. Did something else happen? Are there more rumours? Am I supposed to be married to Lukas Lukas now as well as Sven?"

Mike rubbed his mustache. "Might as well let us both know what we're in for," he told Tank gruffly. "We'll find out for ourselves soon enough."

Tank shrugged. "It's nothing to worry about, really," he said. "Just the usual fans and reporters. But a few of them seem a little worked up about these Sven rumours, that's all. Thought you should be prepared for that."

"Okay," Mike said. "Might as well get out there, then. Time's a-wastin', and we've got places to be."

The huge crowd gathered on the street outside the studio erupted into screams as soon as Star stepped out the door, flanked by Tank and Mike. A row of Swedish police officers stood guard in front of a line of wooden barricades, which were barely containing the eager throngs of people behind them. Here and there, homemade posters waved wildly like sails over the sea of people. Several of the signs were in Swedish, but most were written in English. Star grinned when she noticed one that read SWEDEN LOVES YOU, STAR!

Her smile faded slightly when she spotted another sign nearby. This one read STAR, DUMP THAT LOSER! YOU CAN DO BETTER THAN SVEN!

"Hey," she called to the fan holding it, a dark-haired girl who looked about eleven years old. "You can like me without hating Sven! He didn't do anything bad!"

Star wasn't sure if the girl had heard her, but at her words, a woman standing nearby pushed her way forward to the edge of the police barricade. "Star!" the woman called in a British accent. "Would you like to make a statement about your relationship with Sven Studborg?"

"No comment!" Mike said loudly as Tank put an arm

around Star's shoulders and started to steer her gently towards the waiting car.

But Star resisted his push. "Wait," she told the men. Glancing around, she spotted several other signs denouncing Sven. There were even a couple of posters congratulating the two teens on their rumoured marriage. "We've got a chance to do something about these stupid rumours, right here and now. Shouldn't we do it?"

Mike shook his head firmly. "Leave it alone, Star. You know better. There are always going to be rumours about you – we've talked about this."

"But this time it isn't just about me," Star protested, keeping her voice low so that none of the reporters could hear her words over the shrieks of the crowd. "It's not really fair to Sven to let everyone go on thinking he's some kind of scheming jerk when we could put a stop to it all with just a few words."

Mike stroked his mustache and looked around at the reporters dotted among the fans. "I suppose you're right, darlin'," he said. "And I do see a few decent journalists here along with the usual vultures. Maybe it is better to address it – as long as you're sure you feel up to it?"

Star nodded vigorously. "I'm ready."

"Good." Mike nodded, then stepped away and raised his

arms above his head. "Attention!" he cried. "Could I please have your attention for just a moment?" He glanced helplessly at Tank. "Yo, how do you say 'Shut the heck up' in Swedish?"

Tank grinned and loudly called out to the crowd in Swedish. While the fans weren't silenced entirely – several groups of teen girls seemed completely unable to avoid emitting loud squeals every few seconds, while a chubby teen boy near the front of the crowd continuously crooned several of Star's hit songs in a nasal, off-key voice – most of the onlookers quieted down.

"Thank you," Mike said. "Now, Star will answer a few questions as long as everyone stays polite. Okay?"

Immediately most of the reporters started waving their hands and microphones wildly. "Please! Please!" shouted a tall, thin woman near the curb. "A question over here, please!"

"All right." Mike pointed to her. "What is it?"

The woman smiled at Star. "Miss Calloway, what do you have to say about the stories that have you romantically linked with Sven Studborg? Is there any truth to the rumour?"

Star took a deep breath, quickly but carefully thinking about what she wanted to say. "Not really," she said, her voice carrying clearly over the crowd. "The only truth is that Sven is a new friend of mine, and a very nice guy. I'm honoured that he agreed to open for me on this leg of the tour." She shrugged and glanced around, making sure that everyone could hear her. Reporters and fans alike gazed back eagerly, hanging on her every word. "But we're just friends, that's all."

"Star! Star!" Instantly the hands and microphones were flying again. "Over here, Star!"

With Mike's help, Star answered a few more questions. One reporter asked about that night's concert, but the rest of the reporters wanted to know more about Star and Sven.

How many different ways can I say "We're just friends" before they believe me? she wondered with a sigh. *It's like they're hoping I'll suddenly change my story and admit we're secretly married after all!*

Mike was obviously reaching the same conclusion. "All right, I think that's enough," he called out loudly. "Thank you for your time. Star has to be going now."

Tank steered Star towards the limo at the curb once again, and this time she didn't resist. She waved once more at the crowd, blew a couple of kisses, and then hurried forward to climb into the backseat of the limo. She wasn't sure whether her statements about Sven would make any positive difference in the rumours. But at least she had tried.

Seven

Back at the villa, Lola was waiting in the main room with a spray bottle full of water in one hand and a bag of curlers in the other. "I thought you'd never get here, sugar!" she cried. "I was afraid I was going to have to drag my tired old behind out on that stage myself tonight to keep the audience from rioting."

Star giggled. "Sorry we're late." She plopped into a nearby chair. While Lola quickly dampened her hair and rolled it up into curlers, Star told her about the impromptu press conference, as well as the auditions.

"Sounds like a busy day," Lola mumbled around the bobby pins in her mouth. "Fun, too, except for the icky-rumours part."

She quickly finished rolling Star's hair, then wrapped a silvery turban over it in case Star was spotted or photographed on the way to the concert venue. Once they arrived there, Lola would finish styling Star's hair and apply her make-up as usual.

Tank wandered back into the room and checked his watch. "Are we ready to go?" he asked, seeing Star with her pre-concert turban on. "Believe it or not, we're actually running a few minutes early. We could just hang out here and relax for a little while longer."

Mags and Mike entered from the direction of the kitchen just in time to hear him. "Or perhaps we could get some dinner into this girl," Mags said, her voice stern. "In case the rest of you have forgotten, even pop stars need to eat once in a while."

Lola gasped. "You mean you haven't had dinner yet, baby-doll?" she cried. "We can't have that! You're skinny enough as it is."

"Well, gast my flabber – sorry, sweetheart," Mike added, looking slightly flustered. "I don't know how this happened. I guess I was thinking we would stop somewhere on the way back from the studio, but with all the excitement of our little press encounter, it just plain escaped my mind."

"Don't worry about it," Star said quickly. She knew how upset Mike always got with himself when he slipped up, even though it rarely happened. "I can grab something from the fridge here, and you guys can eat while I'm onstage."

"Forget it," Mags said firmly before the others could

answer. "You've got to eat, and I'm not talking about a bag of truffle-infused gourmet peanuts from the minibar, either. If I'd known ahead of time, I would have cooked something, but it's too late for that now. We'd better call room service and see what they can do for us."

"Do we have time?" Star asked worriedly. "I don't want to be late for the show."

"Mags is right," Mike agreed. "You've got to eat. And don't worry about being late – your fans will wait a few minutes if necessary. Or young Studborg can stretch his set a little longer, maybe."

"That's true," Star said. "Sven has tons of great songs – some he hasn't even had a chance to record yet. I'm sure he could sing the whole night long if he had to."

Mike nodded and checked his watch. "I think we'd better forget room service, though. We can stop on the way to the stadium. I heard about a nice restaurant between here and there that's known to cater to celebs and such. We can call them from the car so they're ready for us."

But by the time they arrived at the restaurant, Mike still hadn't been able to reach anyone there by phone. "Darn it," he muttered, shoving his phone back in his pocket as Tank pulled up to the curb. "Why don't they answer?"

"Well, the lights are on – looks like they're open," Tank said. "Why don't we just see if they have a back room they can clear for us or something? Or even some takeout – we could eat it at the stadium."

"I'll see what I can do."

Mike climbed out of the car and hurried across the sidewalk as the others watched. Before he reached the door, a burly man stepped out and held up his hand warningly.

Star pressed her nose to the window, wishing she could hear what was going on. "It looks like that guy doesn't want to let us in," she commented. "Look at Mike's face – he's getting mad."

She chewed her lower lip worriedly. One of the hardest things to get used to about being famous was not being able to go out to eat like a regular person. If she walked into most ordinary restaurants, she would be mobbed by fans within seconds. So going out to eat meant careful planning, usually arranging ahead of time for the restaurant – or at least a portion of it – to be cleared of other patrons before she arrived. Star had no idea how much extra Mike offered to pay for such service, and she never asked. Although she was starting to get used to such treatment, it still made her feel a tiny bit weird to know that people were willing to go to such lengths to accommodate her just because she was famous.

Mike jogged back towards the limo and signalled for Star to roll down her window. When she did, he gestured towards the burly doorman.

"Let him see who you are," he said. "This jerk doesn't believe it's you in the car."

Mike moved aside, and Star opened the window a little wider. She smiled and waved to the doorman.

The man looked shocked. "Sorry about that, sir," he called in surprisingly good English, seeming agitated. "I'll be right back."

He disappeared inside. A moment later he returned and gestured for them all to come in. Relieved to see that no fans or reporters had noticed them yet, Star hurried into the restaurant lobby with her team surrounding her. The restaurant's manager was waiting there to greet them.

"Sorry about that, Miss Calloway," the manager said. "I'm afraid my doorman didn't believe your manager's story at first." He nodded apologetically in Mike's general direction. "And I had no idea – that is, it's rather a busy night for us, it seems."

For a moment Star had no idea what he was talking about.

When she glanced into the main room of the restaurant, she could see that only one table was occupied. Then she recognized several of the people at the table and gasped.

"Check it out," she whispered to Mike. "It's Jade again!"

Sure enough, the dark-haired teen was sitting there with Stan Starkey and several other members of her entourage. She looked up, recognized Star, and nudged her manager, who glanced around.

Starkey, a stocky man with bad skin and slicked-back black hair, immediately leaped to his feet. "What's the big idea?" he blustered, racing towards the lobby. "I thought this dump was supposed to be closed to the public while my client is here."

The restaurant manager raised his hands soothingly. "I know, sir," he said. "But as you can see, this is not any ordinary member of the public."

Starkey glared at Star. "I know who this is," he spat out, with such venom in his voice that Star took a half-step backward in alarm. "And I don't care. We were here first."

"Let's not be childish, Starkey," Mike said in a dangerously calm voice. "There's plenty of room for all of us. And we'll cross our hearts and swear not to pester Jade for autographs."

Starkey just sputtered, obviously at a loss for words. He

shifted his glare from Star to Mike, and then to the restaurant manager. "Are you going to do something about this or not?" he demanded.

"Please, sir," the manager pleaded. "There is plenty of room. We can seat Star's people on the opposite side of the room if you like. I assure you, my staff will not have any problems serving both parties."

Starkey seemed ready to protest further, but he suddenly seemed to realize it was pointless. Throwing his hands up and muttering under his breath, he stomped back towards his table without another word to the manager or Star's group.

"Nice," Tank commented dryly. "Good to see the ugly American still lives, eh?"

"Never mind," Mike said sharply. "We're not here to fight with him, we're here to eat." He nodded to the manager. "Do you think we'll be able to get in and out of here in half an hour or so? We're in a hurry."

"No problem, sir," the manager said. "Come along and I'll show you to your table."

Soon the group was seated. True to his word, the manager put them across the room from Jade's party. Star was a little disappointed by that. She found herself wishing she could just go over and sit down in the empty chair across from

Jade; she suspected the two of them could be friends if they ever really had the chance to sit down and talk heart to heart. But she knew better than to suggest sitting together. She was afraid that it would only enrage Starkey further – and that he might take his anger out on Jade.

"Too bad Jade's manager is so nasty," she murmured, glancing over at Jade, who seemed to be focused on the plate in front of her.

"I know. Starkey there was so upset to see you it makes me wonder if he might be behind those Sven rumours after all," Mike murmured as he unfolded his napkin. "Then again, maybe he's just being a nasty old cuss as usual."

Star sneaked another glance at Jade. Why did she stay with a manager like that? Star had no idea, but she hoped the other girl came to her senses soon.

The waiters kept them busy for the next few minutes, first taking their orders and then delivering dish after dish of delicious food. It wasn't until she started eating that Star realized how hungry she was. She was careful to order only light, healthy dishes, avoiding many of the tempting treats she'd tried during her lunches with Sven – she didn't want to make herself sick by dancing on a too-full stomach. But she also knew she definitely never would have made it through the whole show on an empty stomach. On especially busy days it was too easy to forget about things like eating and drinking, and she was grateful to her team, especially Mags, for helping her keep track.

Now and then during the meal, Star noticed Starkey shooting disgruntled looks towards her table. But her team ignored him as they chatted about that night's show, Star's friends' upcoming visit, and other topics.

After a while Star saw the people at the other table getting up to leave. Most of the group, including Jade herself, headed straight out to the lobby without a second glance towards Star's table. But Starkey zigzagged between tables until he was standing right in front of them.

"I just want you all to know, there'd better not be so much as a whisper about this dinner in the press tomorrow," Starkey announced abruptly to the table at large. "Jade doesn't need any more of your type of publicity dragging her good name through the mud."

"What sort of publicity would that be, Stan?" Mike asked evenly.

Starkey pursed his fleshy lips and glared at him. "The kind where some pathetic celeb on her fourteenth minute of fame tries to hang on to the limelight by saying or doing anything – like hooking her name to newcomers with real talent, whether they're big international names or local stars."

Star clenched her fists under the table. It wasn't hard to read between the lines of what Starkey was saying. He seemed to think that Star had started those rumours herself just for the free publicity. He was also clearly referring to recent news stories involving a trumped-up feud between Star and Jade.

She wanted to tell Starkey exactly what she thought of that, but she bit her lip and forced herself to keep quiet. Before Mike or anyone else at the table could come up with a response to his outrageous statements, Starkey spun on his heel and hurried away towards the restaurant door.

"Well, *that* was a bit out of line," Tank commented, staring after Starkey as he disappeared from view.

"No kidding!" Star exclaimed. "I mean, *he* was the one who started the stories about me and Jade the last time! How dare he imply it was our fault!"

Mike sighed. "Never mind, sweetheart," he said. "He was just tryin' to rile us. But that does answer one head-scratcher – guess he's not a likely suspect in this latest rash of rumours after all."

"Good point," Mags agreed. "It seems the last thing that unpleasant fellow wants is more publicity for our Star.

Especially after his little plan to use her for publicity fodder for his own artist backfired on him the last time."

"Okay, we know it's not Eddie, and it's not Jade's people either," Star said. "So who is it?"

Nobody seemed to have a good answer. Tank and Lola shrugged, while Mags just stared thoughtfully at her plate.

Mike sighed and picked up his fork. "The truth is, we may never find out," he told Star plainly. "It might have been the work of story-hungry reporters or maybe an overenthusiastic fan." He poked at the remains of his dinner. "Of course, that still doesn't explain that backstage photo . . . ," he muttered under his breath.

Star sighed too, her mind momentarily wandering to her earlier suspicions of Tricia and Lukas Lukas. But she decided not to mention those thoughts – at least not at the moment. Thinking about the whole subject was giving her a headache, and she had to start getting in the mood for her concert. The last thing she wanted to do was allow this latest wrinkle in her life to affect her so much that she ended up disappointing her fans.

Star was only a few minutes late arriving at the concert arena. She rushed backstage and down the hallway to her dressing room, barely pausing long enough to smile at the security guards and other personnel milling around the restricted area.

Mike stopped just outside Star's dressing room, cocking his head towards the stage door down the hall. "Sounds like Studborg's still in the middle of his set," he commented. "That means we have plenty of time. Don't panic, anyone."

"No one's panicking except you, Mike," Lola joked, already pulling items out of the pockets of her make-up apron, which she'd tied on in the limo. "Now come along, babydoll. Let's see if we can make you even more beautiful than you already are."

Star followed her into the dressing room, sipping from the bottle of water Tank handed her while Lola fussed over her hair and make-up. As Dudley went to sleep under her chair, Star stared at herself in the mirror, trying to pump up enthusiasm for the show to come. Part of her was looking forward to the concert as much as ever, but another part was still feeling distracted and unsettled by everything that was happening.

Shake it off, she told herself sternly. *You've got a job to do. You can worry about the other stuff afterwards.*

At that moment Tricia rushed into the room. "Knock

knock!" she sang out. "There you are, Star darling. How are you feeling? Need anything?"

Star barely had time to shake her head before the publicist started off on a monologue about all the wonderful mileage they were getting out of the Sven-related publicity. The more she talked, the more anxious the whole conversation made Star feel.

Could she be the one, like I was thinking before? Star wondered, her stomach clenching into knots at the thought. *If so, Mike's going to be mega-furious when he figures it out. . . .*

Barely bothering to finish her last sentence, let alone say goodbye, Tricia rushed back out of the room again in search of Mike. Star shook her head fiercely as if to shake the suspicious thoughts out of her mind.

"Careful, sugar," Lola warned. "Stop making like a bobble-head. I need to finish your lashes."

"Sorry," Star said. Glancing into the mirror, she saw that her hair and make-up were almost finished. "Is my first costume ready?"

"And waiting," Lola reported. The stylist leaned closer, her warm breath tickling Star's cheek as she carefully dabbed a bit of sparkly mascara on her eyelashes. Then she stood back and smiled. "There!" she said with satisfaction. "Another masterpiece. And in record time, too."

"You're a genius, Lola," Star said with a smile. "Thanks. I'd better get changed – Sven must be almost finished by now."

"I'll go check on that while you change," Lola offered. "Back in a sec."

Star quickly shimmied into her first stage outfit, a midnight blue catsuit decorated with glittery stars. She carefully pulled her star necklace out of the rounded neckline and let it dangle over the dark fabric. Then she touched it and looked into the mirror, thinking about her missing family for a quiet moment as she did before every performance. Keeping them in her mind that way was a private ritual, one she had never shared with anyone, even Mike or Missy. But it helped her feel that she was sharing her current success with the people who had supported her dreams for so long – and who had missed out on seeing most of them come true.

This one's for you guys, like all the rest, she thought, the ghost of a smile passing over her face as she pictured her parents sitting in the audience tonight cheering her on.

Then she took a deep breath and turned away from the mirror. She did a few stretching exercises Tank had taught her to warm up for the dancing she would be doing, then grabbed her water bottle for a few more sips.

Star knew she should be totally focused on the coming show, but she still couldn't seem to quiet her mind. She tried a few meditation tricks Tank had taught her, some deep breathing exercises, and even a few jumping jacks, but nothing worked. She decided to give up and check her e-mail — maybe the familiar activity would settle her enough to help her get her focus back. Besides, the hour was rapidly approaching when her friends would be climbing on a plane way across the ocean, and she still didn't know whether all of them would be coming.

She quickly logged on and clicked open her mailbox. Missy's return address leaped out at her, and she opened the message without daring to guess what it might say. Once again, the text was brief. When she scanned it, Star immediately let out a shriek of joy. Beneath the make-up chair Dudley woke up and leaped to his feet with a bark, banging his round head on a rung.

"What? What's the matter?" Mike came rushing into the room, wild eyed and looking worried.

Star laughed out loud at his expression. "No, no, it's nothing bad," she assured him hurriedly. "I just got an e-mail from Missy, that's all. I'll explain later, but let's just say that my best friend came through — as usual!"

Mike still looked confused, but he shrugged. "Teenagers," he muttered.

Just then Tank hurried in. "It's time," he told Star.

Star reached down to give Dudley a hug for luck. Seconds later she was strapping on her headset and bouncing out into the hall on her way to the stage door. Missy's news had pumped her full of all the energy her other worries had taken from her that day, and then some. She felt as if she were floating at least six feet above the ground.

Just as she approached the stage door, it flew open and Sven leaped through it. His cheeks were pink with the excitement of his just-finished performance, and his blue eyes twinkled brightly.

"How'd it go?" Star cried to him.

"Great!" Sven cried back. "Good luck!"

"Thanks!" Star paused just long enough to trade a high five with him. Then she raced through the door, ready to pour her heart and soul into the performance.

Eight

The next morning Star was afraid she might burst from the excitement of waiting for her friends to arrive. "We should have gone to meet them at the airport," she complained, pacing back and forth in the villa's main room as Mike, Mags, and Lola sat at the dining table finishing their breakfast. Tank had left to pick up the visitors an hour earlier and was due back at any moment.

Mike gazed over at her calmly. "We've been all over this," he said. "That would've been way more hassle than it was worth. Can you imagine the ruckus if you just turned up at the local airport? Tank would really have his hands full then."

Tricia, who had arrived at the villa a few minutes earlier, emerged from the kitchen with a fresh cup of coffee just in time to hear him. "Oh, Mike darling, why didn't you consult with me about this?" she exclaimed loudly. "Star at the airport – that could have provided some lovely photo ops. I would've taken care of everything! Just imagine the press

113

over the sweet images of young Star greeting her childhood pals . . ."

Star hid a grin as Lola and Mags rolled their eyes in unison. Tricia didn't seem to notice.

"But that's water under the bridge, darling," the publicist said, perching on the chair beside Mike's. "I've had some amazing new ideas for publicizing the tour and the album – really creative stuff, if I do say so. Picture this – a weekly newspaper column, written by little Dudley the dog!"

Mike looked decidedly underwhelmed at the idea. He glanced down at Dudley, who was snoozing by his feet. "Uh, I don't think so."

"All right then." Tricia seemed undisturbed by his reaction. "I heard the Platinuminium Corporation is shopping for a new sponsor."

"Platinuminium?" Mags said. "Isn't that a chain of old age homes?"

"Luxury retirement communities, darling," Tricia corrected. "And it might not seem like a perfect fit for Star's image at first, but just think of the opportunity to expand her fan base! Besides, the company really wants to go with someone younger since their last spokesperson died, and I think they'd be willing to cut us a really good—"

"Anybody home?" a familiar voice sang out as the villa's front door swung open.

"Missy!" Star shrieked.

She raced over and flung herself at her best friend, who was standing with two other fourteen-year-old girls in the doorway. Even after not seeing her best friend for weeks, Missy's skinny arms, straight black hair, and braces looked as familiar to Star as her own face.

Laughing, Missy hugged her back. "Nice to see you, too," she said, her words slightly muffled by Star's curly hair. Dudley had awakened from his nap and was dancing around at the girls' feet, barking and drooling happily.

"Hey, don't bogart the pop star!"

Star grinned at the tall, sleek-looking blonde girl pushing forward for her turn. "Shayla!" she squealed. "Wow, I haven't seen you guys in, like, a million years!"

"Yeah, we noticed," put in the third girl, Mandy, who had inherited her soft voice and blue-green eyes from her Caucasian mother and her milk chocolate skin colour and sweet, round-cheeked smile from her African-American father. Star quickly reached out to include her in the group hug.

When she untangled herself from her girlfriends, Star saw

Aaron hanging back behind the others. She gulped, suddenly feeling as if she had three or four left feet and a couple of extra-large noses. She wasn't sure whether to hug him, shake his hand, or just faint on the floor in front of him to avoid the whole problem.

"Hi," she blurted out at last, settling for a welcoming smile. "Uh, I'm glad you're here."

Aaron smiled back uncertainly. "Me too," he said. "I can't believe we're, like, totally in another country and everything."

That made everyone laugh, including Aaron himself, which broke the ice a little. Star quickly pulled her friends inside. Missy had met Star's whole team before, but Star had to make a few introductions for the others. Then she took them all on a tour of the villa.

"Wow," Shayla commented in her usual blunt manner as she surveyed the villa's second-floor bathroom, which featured an extra-large tub and a private sauna. "You really are living it up, Star. Weird to think we all used to share a cabin at summer camp!"

Star laughed. "I know, it's totally weird," she said. "But don't worry, I'm still me — and for the next two and a half days we can just pretend we're all hanging out back at summer camp again. Only with room service and satellite TV!"

Mandy giggled. "Sounds like the best camp ever!"

Star led the way out of the bathroom and down the hall to her bedroom, where she flopped onto the end of her king-size bed. "Okay," she said eagerly. "Now tell me absolutely everything that's happening back home!"

The other girls made themselves at home, settling on the bed or the floor. Aaron looked slightly uncomfortable but finally sat down on a chair near the door.

As her friends started to chatter about the latest New Limpet gossip, Star cast Aaron a worried glance. He hadn't said much since arriving. Somehow Star had thought the two of them would be able to pick up their relationship where they'd left off, just as she was doing with the other girls. But now that he was here, it almost seemed as if they were going to have to start from scratch – again. Not to mention trying to do so in the midst of a gaggle of girlfriends.

But that's okay, she told herself as he caught her looking at him and shot her a brief, shy smile. *At least he's here. And that's something.*

Soon everyone in the group was chatting about their hometown, their other friends, and Star's grandmother, Nans. Hearing about her home made Star miss it – and the people there – more than ever. But she comforted herself with the thought that she would be visiting soon for her grandmother's birthday.

"Anyway, things have definitely quietened down since that last bunch of reporters came around looking for info on your family," Mandy said. "That was really wild – it was like those people wanted to hear any little thing about you and your parents and brother, no matter how silly."

"Yeah, I know," Star said with a sigh. After Jade had given away her secret, reporters had gone crazy trying to dig up more information on the story. "Sorry about that."

Shayla shrugged. "Not your fault, babe," she said. "You can't help it if the whole world wants to know everything about you." She grinned. "You're just lucky you have loyal friends like us to keep all your deep, dark secrets!"

"Star doesn't have any deep, dark secrets," Missy put in loyally.

"Oh yeah?" Star waggled her eyebrows playfully. "Maybe you guys just don't know me as well as you think!"

Mandy rolled her eyes playfully. "Forget it, Star," she said with a giggle. "You're an open book."

Just then Mike stuck his head in the door. "I hate to break up this gossip party, but I'm afraid we've got to get on the road."

"Already?" Star couldn't help being disappointed. But she swallowed it as best she could, not wanting Mike to regret allowing her friends to visit. "Okay. Um, maybe you guys could go sightseeing with Lola or someone, or . . ."

"I've got a better idea." Mike smiled and winked at the visitors. "How would y'all like to find out what a day in Star's life on tour is really like? Because I've arranged for you to come along on her appointments today – we've got a photo shoot, a fancy lunch with some record execs, and a couple of interviews. Oh, and a restaurant opening this evening, followed by a press party. Sound okay?"

"Really?" Mandy gasped as the other two girls shrieked with excitement.

Mike chuckled. "I'll take that as a yes."

Only Aaron looked slightly nervous about the plan. "Are you sure we won't be in the way or something?"

"No, it'll be all right," Star said eagerly, thrilled with Mike's surprise. "This will be great! Thanks a bunch, Mike! Have I ever told you you're the best?"

Mike grinned. "Not so far today."

"Well, you are!" Star gave him a quick hug, then glanced around at her friends. "Come on, let's get going. This is going to be awesome!"

☆ ☆ ☆ ☆ ☆

The rest of the day passed in a blur of activity. First Star and her friends went to a photo shoot for a Swedish magazine. All the girls seemed impressed with the extent of Lola's make-up collection, and Lola good-naturedly did makeovers on all of them while they waited for Star to finish posing.

After that they headed off across town in the limo to have lunch at a snooty French restaurant with some record executives. Luckily, after greeting Star warmly, the record executives seemed much more interested in discussing business with Mike than chatting with her, leaving the teens to their own conversation. Star had to urge her friends to order whatever they wanted to eat – the prices were so high that they were afraid to ask for more than a salad and a glass of water at first. Once she gave the go-ahead, Missy and the other girls quickly got in the spirit, ordering all sorts of unusual and tasty items. Star noticed that Aaron still insisted on a salad, and guessed that he just didn't feel comfortable being so extravagant with someone else's money. To help out, she ordered herself a double order of food and convinced him to help her finish.

When lunch was over it was time for a whole series of interviews. They dashed from radio station to magazine office to TV studio. Star's friends were amazed to notice that at every stop, Star was asked almost the exact same questions – and even more amazed that she managed to sound enthusiastic about her answers each time.

After the last interview the whole group went to a local gym, which was closed to the public while they were there. Star's friends tried to keep up with her workout as Tank guided her through her usual paces, but all of them dropped out within minutes. They went to the juice bar and then played around on the high-tech fitness equipment while Star finished up her routine, which kept her in shape for all the dancing she had to do at her concerts.

Finally they hurried back to the hotel to get changed. That evening Star was scheduled to attend a restaurant opening, followed by a fancy press party being thrown for her by one of the sponsors of her third and final Stockholm concert. Star's friends hadn't brought any really fancy clothes with them, but Lola whipped up outfits for the girls out of spare bits of Star's wardrobe, and she borrowed clothes from a particularly stylish roadie for Aaron. Soon all five friends were dressed up and seated in the limo, along with Tank and Mike. Star's friends peered out at the crowd gathered in front of the restaurant as Tank pulled over to the curb.

"Wow." Mandy's eyes were wide as she stared out the window at the fans waiting for Star. "Is it really like this everywhere you go?"

Star shrugged. "I guess," she said. "I mean, there are usually people waiting for me if they find out where I'm going to be."

"And they usually do, despite our best efforts," Tank put in from the front seat.

Shayla leaned back against the leather seat and sighed. "I don't know how you do it, Star," she said. "How can anyone think celebrities like you have it so easy? After the day we just had, I'm exhausted – and it's not even over yet!"

"Are you going to be okay?" Star asked anxiously. "If you're too tired, Tank could take you back to the hotel."

"Not a chance!" Shayla immediately sat bolt upright and fluffed up her blonde hair. "This could be my only chance to live the life of a supah-star!"

Star giggled. "Okay," she said. "I'd better warn you, as soon as we get out, it will seem like everyone in the world is trying to take our picture."

"Take *your* picture, you mean," Mandy corrected.

"Yeah," Missy agreed. "And don't worry, we already figured that out when everyone wanted to take your picture outside the photo studio, and the radio station, and the magazine offices, and the gym . . ."

"Okay, okay, message received!" Star grinned and gave her best friend a playful shove. "Come on, let's get out there!"

Tank opened the limo door, and Star and her friends got out and hurried along the cordoned-off, red-carpeted pathway into the restaurant. Inside, things weren't much more subdued; it seemed that everyone there wanted to talk to Star or have her sign an autograph. Finally Mike had to pull her away to perform the official ribbon-cutting, and then it was time to rush off again to their next and final stop of the evening.

As they all climbed back into the limo, Star noticed that Aaron was yawning. "Are you okay?" she asked, taking the seat next to him. "I – I feel like I haven't had much of a chance to talk to you and stuff."

Aaron smiled. "It's okay," he said. "I understand. It's nice of you to bring us over for a visit when you're so busy and everything."

"No, it's nice of *you* to be such good sports about all this stuff." Star glanced around to include the rest of the group. "And I'm *never* too busy for my friends. You guys are the coolest!"

They had barely entered the crowded nightclub where the press party was being held when Star spotted Sven pushing towards them through throngs of stylishly dressed party-goers. She smiled and waved to him.

Glancing back at her friends, she saw that they were staring around in awe at the tables groaning with food and the lavish gift bags piled near the door for the guests to take as they left. Mandy was staring up at the stereo speaker hanging from the ceiling above them, which was pumping out one of the songs from Star's latest album. Mike had disappeared into the crowd already, but Tank was hovering behind Star's friends, keeping a watchful eye on the crowd.

"Check it out," Star said, poking Missy in the shoulder to get her attention. "I want you guys to meet a new pal of mine."

Sven reached them a moment later. "*Hej,* Star," he said, raising his voice to be heard above the noise of the people laughing and talking all around them. "I am glad that you are here. Most of these people, they are too old – I am feeling like a child in kindergarten!"

Star laughed. "Sven, these are my friends from back home," she said. "This is Missy, that's Shayla, and Mandy. And this is Aaron."

Sven gave a gallant little bow. "Is it so nice to meet you all," he said. "Any friend of Star is a friend to me as well."

Missy and the other two girls blushed and giggled. Star wasn't surprised. Sven was a lot cuter and more charming than the guys back at New Limpet Middle School.

Well, most of the guys there, anyway . . . She glanced at Aaron. He was staring at Sven uncertainly, not saying anything.

"So, Sven," Missy spoke up playfully. "What's this I hear about you and Star getting married? I can't believe you guys didn't even invite me to the wedding!"

Sven looked confused, then worried. Tank stepped forward and murmured something to him in Swedish, and the young star's face cleared.

"Oh!" he cried, sounding a bit embarrassed. "I am sorry, it is hard for me sometimes to understand a joke in English."

"Don't worry," Shayla spoke up. "It wasn't a very funny joke."

Missy shoved her playfully. "Hey! Don't make me look bad in front of the celebrities."

Sven laughed. "Okay, now I can see why Star is so funny," he said. "It is from hanging around with friends such as you!"

All the girls laughed at that. "Yeah, we totally rock," Shayla agreed with a grin. "If it wasn't for us, Star wouldn't even be cool at all."

"Very funny." Star stuck out her tongue at Shayla. "You wouldn't say that if you heard the mega-cool new song Sven and I wrote together."

"What song?" Aaron asked, speaking up for the first time since entering the party. Star suddenly noticed that his expression was oddly wary.

"Oh, it is a fantastic song!" Sven answered, his blue eyes lighting up with enthusiasm. "We came up with the hook first . . ."

"You mean *you* came up with it," Star corrected him. "It's an awesome riff – it totally made the whole song write itself!"

"Do not be too modest, Star," Sven said. "The lyrics you wrote, they are wonderful! My English would never be good enough to write such a song so quickly."

"Now who's being modest?" Star retorted. "Your English is practically perfect!"

"Perfect?" Aaron broke in with a short laugh. "Um, let's not get carried away here."

Sven looked confused again. "Er, tell him Aaron was just joking," Star muttered to Tank, who nodded and leaned towards Sven.

Meanwhile Star exchanged a worried glance with her girl-friends. She belatedly realized that meeting the handsome, charming Sven might be difficult for Aaron, considering all the rumours. She already thought of Sven as such a good friend that somehow she'd just automatically assumed her old friends would see him the same way. Instead Aaron was being almost rude to the Swedish boy, which was totally unlike him.

I guess he's . . . jealous? Star thought uncertainly, not sure whether to feel more flattered or annoyed by that. *But it's not fair for him to take it out on Sven; he didn't do anything wrong.*

Feeling flustered, she searched her mind for something to say to make everything better. Before she could come up with anything, Aaron shrugged and glared at Sven.

"Whatever," he muttered, just loudly enough for his voice to carry to the whole group. "Star could probably write better songs all by herself."

Star gasped. "Aaron!" she blurted out, shocked at his behaviour.

"Yikes," Shayla murmured under her breath, as Missy and Mandy traded a glance.

Noticing that Sven suddenly looked startled and slightly crestfallen, Star guessed that Tank wouldn't be able to translate them out of this one. Her heart going out to Sven, who was just trying his best to be nice to her friends, she blurted out the first thing she could think of to change the subject and make him feel better.

"Hey, I almost forgot!" She forced a cheerful tone into her voice. "Sven, I wanted to ask what you're doing tomorrow. I'm shooting a video with Lukas Lukas, and I think you'd be perfect for one of the main parts. I meant to ask you about it earlier."

"Oh!" The smile returned to Sven's face. "That sounds wonderful! I will check with my manager."

Star smiled with relief. Then she turned to look at her friends – and gulped as she noticed that Aaron was the one who now looked crestfallen. She kicked herself for not realizing that in trying to make Sven feel better, she might also make Aaron feel even worse.

Not to mention that I have no idea if Lukas Lukas already found someone for that role, she reminded herself, her heart sinking. *Oops. Me and my big mouth.*

Before anyone could say another word, a group of reporters swooped down on the group. Star cast a helpless glance back at Aaron as she was pulled off to talk about her upcoming concert, but he didn't meet her eye. She sighed with frustration, realizing she would have to try to make it up to him later. Right now she had work to do.

By the time the limo pulled up to the villa gate, even Star was yawning. But as she climbed out of the car, she was still thinking about the Aaron situation. She was sure that if she could just get a moment alone with him, she could explain everything and put things back to normal between the two of them.

"Hey," she said softly, grabbing him by the sleeve to hold him back as the others trooped into the villa after Mike and Tank, all of them chattering sleepily about the party and the rest of the day's activities.

Aaron turned to face her. It was dark outside, as clouds shadowed the moon, and she couldn't quite see his expression. She shivered slightly as a chilly breeze rustled the treetops of the garden.

Star cleared her throat, suddenly feeling shy again. "Um, do you want to go for a walk or something?" she asked, her heart beating faster as she looked up at him.

She wasn't only thinking about explaining things to him anymore. The last time the two of them were alone together, they had almost kissed for the first time. Only Tank's untimely interruption had stopped them. Could this be their chance to try again?

"I – I didn't get a chance to show you the courtyard garden earlier," she went on, blushing furiously under the cover of darkness and hoping he couldn't read her mind. "We could take a look around out there now if you're not too tired."

For a second Aaron didn't answer. Then he shrugged. "Maybe some other time," he said in a flat, disinterested voice. "I'm pretty beat."

Star leaned back, surprised and a little hurt by his abrupt response. Before she could figure out what to say next, Aaron had hurried into the villa, leaving Star all alone in the chilly darkness.

Nine

"I still can't believe we had to get up so early," Shayla moaned, swallowing yet another yawn. "I thought you music superstars were supposed to sleep until noon every day."

Star grinned at her. "Sorry to burst your bubble."

"Hey, quit complaining," Missy told Shayla. "How often do we get to hang out at a real, live video shoot?"

"Good point," Aaron said, glancing around the warehouse-like main shooting studio of Lukas's facility, which was full of all sorts of interesting props and scenery. "This is pretty cool."

Star smiled uncertainly, glad that he seemed to be in a better mood. Still, she couldn't help noticing that he hadn't looked her in the eye all morning. Once again she wished she could just pull him aside and make him understand that there was nothing between her and Sven – or her and anybody else. Instead of bringing them closer, she was afraid that this visit was ruining whatever sort of relationship she and Aaron had.

"Ready to get your face on, sugar?" Lola asked, hurrying over to the group. "Lukas wants to get rolling pretty soon."

"I hope he's not upset that you brought us," Mandy commented. "We'll try not to get in the way."

"In the way? Nonsense, young lady!" Lukas Lukas himself appeared suddenly behind them. "I heard that Star's young American friends were here, but I never expected them to be such lookers! Hubba hubba! Please say that all of you gorgeous young people will agree to appear in the video as extras! It would mean the world to me."

Star hid a grin as her friends goggled speechlessly at the odd-looking director, whose hair was wilder and bushier than ever. "They'd totally love that, Mr Lukas," she answered for them. "Right, guys?"

"Right!" Missy and Shayla chorused. Aaron and Mandy continued to look stunned but nodded vigorously.

"Wonderful! I'll expect you all on the set in twenty minutes sharp." The director turned away and called out something in Swedish to one of the many techs scurrying about.

"This is so cool!" Shayla squealed. "Is he really going to put us in your video, Star?"

"Sure!" Star laughed at her friends' excited expressions.

Aaron looked nervous. "Maybe I'll just watch you guys," he said. "I always look weird on camera."

"Forget it!" Shayla said. "If we're doing it, you're doing it too."

The other girls backed her up, and finally Aaron shyly agreed to give it a try. "But if I look weird in front of the whole world, it's your fault," he added with a slightly nervous smile.

Missy was almost hopping up and down with excitement. "Lola, you've got to help make us up," she begged. "Please? I don't want to look like a dork in my first video appearance!"

Lola chuckled. "Come along with me, chickadees," she commanded, leading the way towards a dressing room area at one end of the huge room. "Let's see what we can do."

As Lukas Lukas called "Cut!" and started chattering at the cameramen in Swedish, Star sneaked a peek at the clock on the wall. She had called Lukas Lukas during the press party the night before to tell him about her impulsive invitation for Sven to be in the video. The director had been delighted at the idea, and had promised to contact Sven's manager immediately to make arrangements.

Now it was almost time for Sven to arrive to shoot his scenes. How would Aaron react?

"Star!" Lukas Lukas barked, breaking into her worried thoughts. "Over here, please, my dear. We're going to shoot the first part of the sock hop scene now."

"Okay." Star headed for the portion of the studio that was made up to look like a fifties-era diner. She was already wearing her costume for the scene – a poodle skirt and a ponytail. Her background dancers, her friends from home, and the other extras were dressed in period outfits as well. The director had just finished filming a couple of test shots with some of the extras, including Star's friends.

Star gave Missy and the others a quick wave. Suddenly Lola swooped down on her, wearing her make-up apron. "Let me just touch up your eyeshadow," the stylist said, already reaching for Star's face.

As Star patiently waited for the stylist to finish, Lukas Lukas hurried towards her again. "I have just had a brainstorm, my dear," he announced. "What can be more a sign of the American fifties than an American fifties car? I have decided we will have you open this scene by driving into the diner, then beginning to dance atop the hood of the car. Luckily one of my assistant directors has the perfect car for the job."

He waved one hand at the oversized doors at one end of the studio. Someone had just opened them, and now a bright red, low-slung car with shiny chrome and shark fins was driving slowly through the opening.

Star's eyes widened. "What?" she exclaimed. "Are you serious? But – but I'm only fourteen. I don't have a driver's license. I don't really even know how to drive."

The director seemed unconcerned. "It will all be fine," he announced. "Finish with your make-up, then we will begin."

Star gulped and nodded. "I'll be right there."

Driving turned out to be both harder and more fun than Star would have guessed. The first few times she tried to put the car into gear, she wound up merely causing a terrible screeching sound to emerge from somewhere under the hood. She caught the car's owner, a pretty young dark-haired woman, wincing a few times.

She was aware that her friends from home were watching and laughing hysterically. Star grinned sheepishly over at them, realizing that she was giving them some excellent stories to tell when they got home. She just hoped they didn't tell Nans too much about it – she worried about Star enough as it was.

Mostly, though, she was glad that her friends were having as much fun as she was. Even Aaron seemed to be relaxing.

"Better make sure your tutor starts working on driver's ed now, Star," he called jokingly as the car wobbled past him a few minutes later.

"Ha ha," she called back, trying desperately to avoid crashing into a pillar.

She stomped on the brake just in time, then leaned back with relief. A figure hurried up to the car.

"Are you okay, Miss Star?" an accented voice asked. "I can with the car help you, if you please. To turn it around for you?"

Glancing up, Star recognized the awkward young man, Lars, from the auditions. In all the excitement of the past couple of days, she had forgotten all about him.

"Oh!" she exclaimed. "Lars! I just realized – I think I accidentally made your part in this video smaller. See, I asked my friend Sven Studborg to be in it, and I think he's going to play the part Lukas had planned for you. I'm so sorry! I know how excited you were about it."

She felt a little guilty, especially since she hadn't even thought about Lars until that moment. But he smiled happily.

"It is no matter, Miss Star," he said. "I understand in total.

Sven Studborg, he is most handsome and talented. I am most happy merely to have a part at all, even in the background."

Star smiled with relief. "Thanks for understanding," she said. "Um, now if you'd really like to help me get this car turned around . . ."

Finally Lukas Lukas decided he had enough shots of Star driving. "We will shoot the hood-dancing part a little later," he said. "After we clean up a few of the marks left on the car from the scenery collisions."

Star smiled sheepishly. "Sorry about that," she said. "I did warn you I couldn't drive. I'm sure my manager will pay for any damage or whatever."

"Never mind, my dear." The director smiled. "You did marvellously."

That seemed like an exaggeration to Star, but she smiled back. "Thanks."

As the director turned away to direct some assistants who were setting up the scenery, Star's friends wandered over. "Nice driving, babe," Shayla said with a grin. "I hope you weren't expecting to get your licence before age, oh, thirty-five or so."

"What does she need a licence for?" Missy hooked a thumb towards Star's bodyguard, who was sipping a soda a few feet away. "She's got Tank to drive her around anywhere she wants to—"

"Star! Oh, Miss Star!" a breathless voice interrupted.

Star turned and saw Lars rushing towards her. She greeted him and introduced him to her friends.

"It wonderful is to meet you all," Lars said. He held up his mobile phone. "If you please – I wonder if one of you would so kind be as to photograph my picture with Star? It would be my greatest dream come true!"

"Sure," Star said. "Hey Aaron, could you take our picture?"

"No problem." Aaron seemed pleased to be asked. He took Lars's phone and quickly figured out how to take a picture with it. "Okay, say cheese . . ."

As Star smiled into the camera, she heard Lukas Lukas bustling about nearby. "Now it is almost time to start with the scenes within the diner," the director called out. "Is our leading man here yet?"

"Right here, sir!"

Still grinning into the camera as Aaron took a couple more shots of her and Lars, Star saw Sven hurrying across the studio towards them. The young singer looked even more handsome than usual in blue jeans and a black leather jacket, with his blond hair slicked back from his forehead.

Her stomach jumping nervously as she glanced at Aaron, Star gave Sven a quick wave. "Hi there!" she called.

Instead of answering, Sven frowned as he spotted the little group around Star. "What are you doing here?" he snapped.

For a second Star thought he was speaking to Aaron. Then she realized that he was staring at the man next to her.

"Sven!" Lars cried. Then he broke into a torrent of rapid Swedish.

Star blinked. "Wait," she said as Sven marched towards Lars. "Do you two know each other?"

"I am afraid so," Sven replied grimly. He glared at Lars and began yelling at him in Swedish.

Star glanced hopelessly over at Tank. "What's going on?"

Tank was listening carefully. "Sounds like they know each other very well," he said. "In fact, if I'm not mistaken, I think Lars is Sven's old manager!"

"Huh?" Star vaguely recalled Sven – or had it been Mike? – mentioning that the young Swedish star had recently changed managers.

Sven looked over at her. "Oh, I am sorry," he said in English. "I am being rude. It is just such to a shock, to find

Lars here." He glared at Lars. "Now tell me, what are you doing here?"

Lars shrugged. "I am needing work since you sack me," he said. He added a few words in Swedish, sounding irritated.

"He says it wasn't his fault," Tank translated. He wrinkled his brow. "I'm not sure what he means by that."

At that moment Star heard Lukas Lukas calling her name as well as Sven's. "Yikes," she said, not wanting to leave until she knew what was going on. But she didn't have much choice. "Listen, Tank, see if you can get to the bottom of this, okay?"

"Yes," Sven added icily. "I would like to know more about this as well."

Star hurried towards the director with Sven at her heels and the rest of her friends trailing behind them. She glanced over her shoulder just in time to see Tank take Lars firmly by the shoulder and usher him away.

By the time the scene was finished, Tank had uncovered the whole story.

"It seems Lars there is the one who started those rumours about you guys," he told Star, who was perched on a stool sipping some water while Lola rearranged her hairdo for the next shot. "He knew some of the security staff at the stadium, and they thought he was still with Sven. That's how he got in and snapped that photo of you two." He shrugged. "I guess giving it to the press was supposed to be some sort of revenge against Sven for firing him or something. He gave it to some hometown paper – didn't know it would blow up into an international incident. Or so he says, anyway."

Mike was standing nearby listening carefully, along with Sven and the rest of Star's friends. "He'll be sorry he pulled a stunt like that," the manager growled.

For a second Star was inclined to agree with him. Lars's stunt had caused her and her friends a lot of grief over the past few days. She still wasn't sure how she and Aaron were going to get past it.

Then she recalled Lars's goofy enthusiasm at the video audition, along with the little Sven had told her about his old manager. It was easy to think of Lars as a cold-hearted, scheming villain – like a Swedish version of Stan Starkey. But while Star was certain that Starkey had known exactly what he was doing when he revealed Star's secret to the world, she was equally sure that Lars had never meant her any harm at all. The more she saw of him, the more she suspected that he hadn't even really meant to hurt Sven. All he'd wanted was some attention, like a big, clumsy dog knocking over furniture in his eagerness to be petted. Thinking of Lars that way made Star feel more pity than anger.

"Don't be too mad at him, Mike," she said, shooting a glance at Lars, who was standing alone about fifty yards away watching some techs fiddle with a camera.

Mike looked surprised. "What?" he said. "Now darlin,' I know you're soft-hearted, but . . ."

"No, really," Star interrupted. "I know he wasn't very good at his job, and it wasn't a very nice thing to do. But I feel sort of sorry for him. I mean, the poor guy doesn't have a clue, but he seems so totally enthusiastic about the music business."

"Yes, he is," Sven put in. "That is his only talent, is the enthusiasm, unfortunately. He means well, he is just rather, um, what is the English word?" He glanced at Tank.

"A loser?" Tank supplied helpfully.

Sven smiled. "That will do," he agreed.

"So maybe we should just forgive him." Star smiled at Sven. "Don't you think? I know he caused us a lot of trouble, but we'll get past it. As far as I'm concerned, he can even stay in the video if he wants – as long as he promises never to pull something like this again."

Sven looked dubious, but then broke into a smile himself. "You are something, Star," he said. "Really a special person."

Star was relieved . . . until she looked around and noticed Aaron frowning at her. Before she could include him in her smile, he quickly looked away.

Why can't he just get over it? she wondered, caught between worry and frustration. *What more can I do to prove that he's the only guy for me?*

The next scene on the schedule was set in the 1920s. Star wore a cute flapper dress, while Sven was in a flashy matching suit.

"Okay, does everybody know what they are to do?" Lukas Lukas asked. He repeated his question in Swedish. "All right, then. From the top. Action!"

Music poured from the speakers. Star grabbed Sven by both hands, and the two of them started to dance. Even though they'd both only learned the steps about fifteen minutes earlier from Lukas Lukas's choreographer, they were both experienced dancers and didn't miss a step. Star was still worried about Aaron – she wished there was something she could do to convince him of her feelings once and for all – but within seconds she had caught the spirit of the music and was enjoying herself thoroughly. Sven was a good dancer, and she could see the background dancers following their moves all around them. At the back of the set, her friends and the other extras were clapping along enthusiastically. As Sven spun her around, she caught a glimpse of Aaron standing with the others, smiling and clapping. But she couldn't tell whether his smile was real or just pasted on for the cameras.

Soon the dance sequence neared its end. Sven was supposed to spin Star around once more, then stop, drop to one knee, and kiss her hand to finish the scene.

The bright lights of the set blurred as Sven spun her. Star quickly picked a focus point to keep from getting dizzy – Aaron's face. As she watched him, she saw that he was staring straight back at her for the first time all day. She couldn't quite read his expression, and suddenly she was tired of trying. Why did the two of them spend so much time and energy being shy and trying to second-guess each other's every thought and feeling?

I like him, he likes me, and everyone knows it, she thought. *Maybe it's time we just went with that and stopped being so silly. It's not like we have tons of time to spend together as it is – why waste the time we have?*

As Sven caught her around the waist to end the spin, Star kept her gaze on Aaron rather than looking up at her partner as she was supposed to. A sudden impulse had just grabbed her.

She pulled away from Sven, who jumped backwards in surprise. Racing past several pairs of background dancers, the fringe of her dress shimmering as she ran, she skidded to a stop in front of a surprised-looking Aaron.

With a grin she grabbed him by the hand and pulled him forward into full view of the cameras. Before anyone could react – Lukas Lukas, Sven, or even Aaron himself – she grabbed him with both arms and stretched up to plant a big kiss on his cheek.

"Wha – why – uh—" Aaron stammered, clearly at a loss for words. His entire face was slowly turning beet red.

At that moment the music segment ended. "Cut!" Lukas Lukas cried.

Star let go of Aaron and glanced over at the director, realizing that Lukas Lukas would probably be angry with her for messing up the carefully choreographed scene. To her surprise, he was smiling broadly.

"That was wonderful!" the director cried, clapping his hands. "Very inventive and unexpected. I love it! We will do it again, just the same way, to make sure we have all the angles, *ja*?"

Everyone else on the set laughed and started applauding. Star took a playful little bow, and after a quick poke in the side, Aaron did the same.

"What did you do that for?" he asked softly.

Star smiled at him. "I just felt like it," she whispered back. "Was it okay?"

Aaron was still blushing, but now he was smiling, too. "It was okay," he whispered. "Very, very okay."

Star felt like bursting into song as she moved into position for the second take. She would remember the look in Aaron's eyes just then for a long time. It wasn't exactly a long, deep, soul-searching conversation, but she had the feeling he was starting to understand that she really did care about him. And for the moment, at least, that would do.

Ten

"I think this is his last song," Star whispered to Mike, craning her neck through the backstage door and listening to Sven, who was out onstage.

Mike nodded. "Think you're right," he said. "Better get on up there and be ready. Knock 'em dead, okay?"

"Definitely." Star grinned, then tiptoed up to the edge of the stage.

She waited there, just out of sight of the sold-out crowd, until the final notes of Sven's song faded. She heard him speaking into the microphone in Swedish. Then he switched to English.

"And now," he said, his words echoing through the packed stadium. "I like to introduce you all to a dear friend of mine – Miss Star Calloway!"

The place exploded with excitement as Star leaped forward, bouncing out onto the stage. She waved to the crowd, even though the spotlights made it hard to see anything beyond the edge of the stage.

"Hi there, Stockholm!" she cried into her headset. "How's it going?"

Without waiting for the cheers to fade, Sven turned and signalled to his band. "Let's hit it, guys," he called.

Music poured out of the speakers. Star smiled as she listened to the opening riff of their brand-new song, "Together We Can Do It." It sounded great!

She and Sven stepped forward and started to sing. They'd only had a short time to practice the new number before the concert, but that turned out to be enough. They traded off some lines, harmonized on the chorus, and sang other parts in unison as if they'd been rehearsing for months.

As her eyes adjusted to the bright lights, Star spotted Aaron and her other friends sitting right in the middle of the front row. She jumped forward and waved to them. Then she kneeled down as the song reached a new verse, singing directly to Aaron:

"We have to stick together, 'cuz we hate to be apart," she sang, her voice ringing out clearly as Sven stepped back for a moment. "Being with you just feels right, deep down inside my heart . . ."

Sven stepped forward and took over again, but Star hardly noticed. All she could see was Aaron smiling up at her. She grinned back, momentarily forgetting that they were surrounded by thousands of people.

Then she snapped out of it, joining in to sing the next chorus. But as the song ended, her gaze wandered back towards Aaron. She saw that he was standing on his seat, yelling and clapping even more enthusiastically than everyone else. She grinned and blew him a kiss, causing the fans sitting nearby to scream excitedly.

She backed away out of sight of the audience, glancing behind her as her band and stage crew scurried onstage and started setting up. Sven was speaking to the crowd again in Swedish, though she had no idea how they could hear him over the screams.

I guess they liked the song, she thought happily. I can't wait to get together with Sven again and record it!

The two of them had already started making plans to do just that. It made Star feel a little less sad about leaving Sweden the next day. She would miss Sven a lot, but by now she was sure that they would always be friends.

She tried not to think about how much she was going to miss Aaron, Missy, and the others when they left the next morning. . . . Pushing aside those thoughts, she moved into position and waited for the stage crew to finish their work so she could start her show.

"I can't believe we're leaving already," Missy moaned, dropping her suitcase on the floor near the villa's front door. "We just got here!"

"I know." Star gave her best friend a hug. "But I'll see you soon. I'm coming home for Nans's birthday, remember?"

Nearby, Shayla was staring at the television, which was turned to PopTV. "Hey, they just did a story about you and Sven," she called to Star. "Or rather, about how there is no you and Sven after all. I guess somebody at the network finally, like, hired a fact-checker or something and figured it out."

"Why didn't you tell us?" Mandy complained.

"Didn't have time," Shayla replied. "If I'd blinked, I would've missed it myself. Now they're back to talking about Jade's manager's fight with Lukas Lukas again."

Star rolled her eyes. After the concert they'd all heard that Stan Starkey had managed to insult Lukas Lukas somehow. Now the director was refusing to work with Jade after all.

"That's always the way," Tank commented, hoisting several

of the visitors' suitcases in one hand as if they weighed nothing. "The juicy stuff gets nonstop coverage, and the
retractions and corrections get slipped in as quickly as possible."

"Show business," Mike said succinctly. He checked his
watch. "Okay, gang. You all need to leave for the airport in
exactly fifteen minutes. So grab another glass of OJ or whatever – y'all have a long trip in front of you, and so do we."

As Star took a sip of orange juice, Aaron sidled over to her.
"Hey," he said quietly. "Um, I never did get a look at that
courtyard garden. Maybe you could show me around there
now – if you want to, that is."

Star was so surprised that she almost dropped her glass.
Ever since that special moment at the concert the night
before, she could tell by Aaron's behaviour that things were
definitely back to normal between them – at least as normal
as they'd ever been. But Star had been so busy since then that
they hadn't had a moment alone.

"Sure," she said, suddenly too tongue-tied to say anything
more.

She led the way out a side door, and they found themselves
in the garden. It had rained earlier that morning, leaving the
plants and walkways glistening in the sunlight that filtered

through the treetops. They walked a little way in silence, enjoying the beauty and peacefulness of the courtyard.

Finally Aaron spoke. "Hey," he said quietly. "Uh, thanks for inviting me to come here. It was fun. And I'm sorry if I acted sort of, you know, weird. Or whatever."

"I understand." Despite his garbled words, Star did. "And it's totally okay. I'm sorry you had to put up with all that Sven stuff. You know, the rumours."

"That's all right." Aaron glanced over and smiled shyly.

Star took a deep breath. "Sometimes – sometimes I wish my life was more normal, you know?"

"Me too," Aaron admitted. "But I guess if it was, you wouldn't be you." He reached over and took her hand in his own.

Star's heart started beating faster. She squeezed his hand, and he squeezed back.

"I'm really glad you came," she said. "I think about you a lot."

"Really?" Aaron sounded surprised. "I – I think about you, too. All the time."

"Really?"

Star couldn't think of anything else to say. But all of a sudden, that seemed perfectly okay. They had drifted to a stop, and now she turned to face him. He looked back at her.

Her heart was racing so fast she was afraid it might explode. But somehow the usual awkwardness was gone. When he put his hands on her waist, she shivered slightly, but it felt surprisingly normal and natural to put her hands on his shoulders.

She tilted her head back to look into his eyes. He was looking back at her. This time he didn't look away – and this time, thankfully, Tank was nowhere in sight. Aaron leaned closer, closer . . .

Star let her eyes drift shut. A second later she felt his lips brush against hers.

The kiss – their very first real kiss – lasted a nice, long time. Finally they pulled away and looked at each other. They were both blushing, but smiling as well. Neither of them spoke, and Star was ready to let the wonderful, breathless, silent moment go on as long as possible – maybe forever.

"Star?" Tank's voice called from somewhere close by, shattering the magical mood. "You out here?"

Star blinked, startled. Aaron quickly dropped his hands from her waist and took a step back.

"Oops," Star said, once again wishing that her life wasn't

quite so hectic. She glanced towards the door to the villa, which was hidden behind a line of shrubs. At least Tank hadn't actually interrupted them this time! "I guess that means it's time for you guys to go."

"Guess so," Aaron said. He cleared his throat, looking nervous, dejected, and happy at the same time. "I'll miss you, Star. A lot."

"Me too," she said softly.

Without another word they started walking back towards the door. Star's heart was already aching at the thought that Aaron would be climbing into that limo any minute now. She touched her star necklace, suddenly feeling a little lonely, even though he was still right there beside her.

But despite her sadness, there was a little song of happiness singing away inside her heart. She knew that the memory of her first kiss would help keep that song going until she saw him again.

Catch Star's next act

Blast from the Past

During her tour of Switzerland, a girl named Samantha introduces herself to Star and explains that she and Star went to kindergarten together before Sam's family moved away to Europe. Star doesn't really remember Sam, but Sam seems to have lots of fond memories of Star's parents, and that's a topic Star never gets tired of discussing.

Soon Star and Sam are virtually inseparable. But Mike and Mags are suspicious of Star's friend's motives. Is Sam really a blast from Star's past, or is she after something more than memories?

**Find out in *Blast from the Past*,
the next book in the Star Power series!**

She's sharp.

She's smart.

She's confident.

She's unstoppable.

And she's on your trail.

MEET THE NEW NANCY DREW

Still sleuthing,

still solving crimes,

but she's got some new tricks up her sleeve!

NANCY DREW

girl detectiv